Even If This Love Disappears Tonight

Misaki Ichijo

YEN
ON
NEW YORK

Even If This Love Disappears Tonight

Misaki Ichijo

Translation by Winifred Bird
Cover photo by Koichi

KONYA, SEKAI KARA KONO KOI GA KIETEMO
©Misaki Ichijo 2020
First published in Japan in 2020 by KADOKAWA CORPORATION, Tokyo.
English translation rights arranged with KADOKAWA CORPORATION, Tokyo through TUTTLE-MORI AGENCY, INC., Tokyo.

English translation © 2022 by Yen Press, LLC

Yen On
150 West 30th Street, 19th Floor
New York, NY 10001

Visit us at yenpress.com ✳ facebook.com/yenpress ✳ twitter.com/yenpress
yenpress.tumblr.com ✳ instagram.com/yenpress

First Yen On Edition: December 2022
Edited by Yen On Editorial: Shella Wu, Ivan Liang
Designed by Yen Press Design: Wendy Chan

Yen On is an imprint of Yen Press, LLC.
The Yen On name and logo are trademarks of Yen Press, LLC.

Library of Congress Control Number: 2022038171

ISBNs: 978-1-9753-4833-5 (paperback)
       978-1-9753-4834-2 (ebook)

10 9 8 7 6 5 4 3 2 1

LSC-C

Printed in the United States of America

CONTENTS

A beautiful girl who was supposed to have meant nothing to me once said this:

"We can date, but only under three conditions. First, don't talk to me until after school. Second, when we contact each other, we keep it short. And third, don't fall in love with me. Can you do those three things?"

Back then, there was a lot I didn't understand. On a practical level, how to tell a girl I liked her when I didn't. On a philosophical level, death. On a poetic level, love.

And then I added another thing to the list. Myself.

For some reason, I told this girl I didn't know yes.

An Unknown Boy
and His Unknown Girl

1

I used to think I'd live my whole life without surprising myself. I thought I would never be the type of person who would do something and think, *Hey, that wasn't like me*, or *I can't believe I just did that*. The same went for tests and grades. I was never surprised by how well or poorly I did. I never underestimated or overestimated myself. But that day after school, I surprised myself.

Shortly after the new school year started, a couple of guys in my class started harassing another boy. They were probably venting their anger about having worked hard to enter a public college-preparatory high school to then only end up in the non-advanced class in our second year. I understood their feelings, but I couldn't sympathize with them.

The victim of their bullying sat in front of me.

Although I didn't intentionally avoid making friends, I spent a lot of my time in class reading, and I didn't go out of my way to get involved with people. But I couldn't stand watching a decent guy suffer right in front of me.

"What's the point of doing that?" I finally asked them one day when they were up to their usual antics.

The whole classroom went silent. The ringleader turned around and sneered at me. That was the moment I became their new target. *Figures*, I thought indifferently.

Everything up to that point was fine.

I couldn't have cared less about the childish horseplay, baseless rumors, or scornful jeers. They must have gotten bored when I ignored them, because they eventually shifted their focus back to the other boy.

This time, they did things more discreetly. I heard they even extorted money from him. Not long after, he started skipping school.

I told them to cut it out. I didn't raise my voice, but I was angry.

"Fine. Do one thing for me, and I'll stop," the ringleader said.

I told him I would. I knew it was going to be bad, but his order was like something a junior high schooler would ask for.

"Go tell Maori Hino in Class 1 you like her. Today," he said.

That day after school, I stopped her in the hall. I asked her to go behind the school with me, as instructed, and did what he'd asked while he secretly watched. I figured I'd explain it to her later and apologize.

"We can date, but only under three conditions," she said.

I never imagined she'd go along with it. She raised her fingers one by one, listing off each condition. I was so shocked, I could hardly talk. I'm sure the guys who were watching were equally stunned, too.

I didn't know much about Hino. She was in the advanced class. Apparently, a lot of guys thought she was hot. I'd heard a couple of my classmates talking about her before. I took a better look at her.

She was beautiful, sure, but she didn't mean anything to me.

If I said no to her conditions, she probably would have flipped her long black hair, said, "Fine, we'll pretend this never happened," and walked off. I wonder if it would have been better to just let everything end neatly.

"Okay."

My voice didn't sound like my own. That was my first thought. My second thought was *Why did I just say that?*

I couldn't believe what I'd just done.

She could probably tell that I hadn't meant it when I said I liked her. But her tense expression suddenly relaxed, and, to my surprise, she smiled.

"Okay. So starting tomorrow, we're girlfriend and boyfriend," she said before turning around and starting to walk away like her business was done.

Then she paused and turned back with a faint smile that looked natural but not eager, like a true reflection of her personality.

"By the way, what was your name? Could you tell me again?"

"Ah, um, it's Tooru. Tooru Kamiya."

"Oh, I remember now. That's right. It's Tooru. I'm Maori Hino. Let's talk tomorrow after school. And one more thing. I would really appreciate it if you could keep the fact we're dating to yourself. Well, bye."

She smiled again and walked off. This time she didn't look back.

The group of bullies who'd been hoping to watch me be rejected came out of their hiding spot looking disappointed.

"What the hell's wrong with you?" said the ringleader, who I'm sure had been waiting for the perfect chance to laugh at me.

"I just did what you told me to do," I replied simply.

The atmosphere grew ominous. He glared at me and snorted, then walked past me, banging into my shoulder as he went. The other guys looked like they wanted to say something but silently followed him instead. I watched them go, then turned in the direction Hino had left in.

I'd never had a crush on anyone in my class before. I've got a classic case of what people call a "sister complex." I adored my older sister like a mother, and I always figured my dad and I would live together, just the two of us, while we waited for her to come back.

I honestly believed that's how my life would go.

Because of my family situation, I knew I would have to get a job straight out of high school instead of going to university. I'm pretty sure that's part of the reason I was put in the non-advanced class this year. I'd never paid attention to the girls in my class, even after starting high school, although it wasn't exactly because I saw us having different futures. Maori Hino was just another girl I didn't pay any mind to.

I wondered if I should chase after her and tell her I'd been forced into this fake confession. Though it would be awkward to say that after accepting her conditions for dating. She'd said we could talk tomorrow. I figured I might as well wait till then. Maybe by then my thoughts would be clearer. I started walking home, looking up at the twilight sky.

That was how the two of us met.

2

The first thing I do in the morning is wash our clothes.

I live in a public housing complex with my dad. I do most of the housework. Maybe I don't need to do the laundry every day, since it's just him and me. But after my sister left, I wanted to keep up her routines. Like she always used to say, it's important to keep things sanitary. We might be poor, but she always made sure Dad and I had ironed handkerchiefs and clothes that weren't frayed, stretched out, or stained.

The important thing isn't to have a facade of cleanliness; it's to make being sanitary part of our daily lives. That's another thing my sister used to say a lot. When I think about it now, she might have said that to protect our family from shabbiness.

I hung up the laundry and was making our breakfast and bentos when Dad got up and poked his head into the living room.

"Morning, Tooru. What's for breakfast?"

"Morning, Dad. Before I tell you, how about finally shaving that beard of yours?"

Dad doesn't look especially sanitary at first glance. He takes care of himself, but his stubbly face undoes all his efforts. He works the assembly line at a car factory near our house. He doesn't work nights, and the pay is lower because of that.

My mom died when I was little. Back when she was alive, I feel like he had the sort of ambition you'd expect from a dad, but not anymore. A lot of our relatives say he really changed after Mom died.

Dad sat down with me to eat breakfast. I finished first and put the rest of our lunches together before washing up the dishes. I grabbed my schoolbag and my bento, said goodbye to Dad, and headed out. I didn't forget my handkerchief.

The May sky was high and blue. The month was almost over, but I like May. It probably has to do with the story my sister made up about "May sickness." It referred to college freshmen who start school in

April and feel listless by May. She told me that by then, the cherry blossoms have fallen, and the busiest time of year is over, so everyone feels more relaxed. You can sit around looking at the fresh leaves, and people become a little lazy. According to her, that's what "May sickness" was. Such an elegant lie.

My sister was as gentle and quiet as a tree. Except now and then, she would tell me a completely straight-faced lie like that.

I thought about the past as I walked to the station. At the park on the way there, I found some especially brilliant green leaves. I was so moved that I wished I could have left my heart there while I went on to school.

May sickness. So elegant.

"That's really interesting, Kamiya, but I think Wataya has been staring at us for a while."

It was break time after second period. I was telling Shimokawa, the guy who sits in front of me, about May sickness when he abruptly pointed out the girl in the hallway.

"Look, over there," he prodded.

I turned around. A beautiful but grumpy-looking girl was standing there. It was Hino's friend Wataya. A bunch of our classmates were giving her confused stares as she peered into our classroom.

I'd never talked to her. Like Hino, she seemed unrelated to my life. I'd heard she was quite smart, and she had a secret following of guys who adored her cold beauty.

The day before, when I'd stopped Hino in the hallway after school, Wataya had been standing next to her. She hadn't followed when I told

Hino I wanted to talk to her behind the school, but she'd looked at me like I mystified her.

"I guess I forgot to mention that I told Hino I liked her yesterday," I mumbled, looking back at Shimokawa.

"What? You did? Why?" he asked, turning away from Wataya.

Shimokawa had been absent yesterday, so this was the first he'd heard of it. Before I answered, I glanced at the group of popular guys in our class. When I caught the eye of the one who'd ordered me to approach Hino, he looked away with a bored expression.

So far that morning, they hadn't harassed Shimokawa. They seemed to be keeping their promise.

I glanced at the hallway again. My eyes met Wataya's. She had short hair that looked great on her and a symmetrical face that was hard to read. Although, I'm hardly one to talk when it comes to poker faces.

I saw her mouth form the word *um*. Considering how she was close with Hino, she might have heard what had happened the day before. I didn't want to attract too much attention, so I stood up before she had a chance to call out my name.

"Sorry, Shimokawa. I'll be back in a minute," I said.

"What? Oh, uh, okay."

I walked toward Wataya, then right past her. She turned toward me with a suspicious look. I pointed to a corner of the hallway. She must have gotten the message since she followed me quietly.

"Sorry. Did you want to talk to me?" I asked once we'd made it to a relatively empty spot.

"It's Kamiya, right?" she asked curtly.

I nodded. "And you're Wataya, I believe?"

"Yeah. I don't think we've ever really talked before. I had a hard time finding you."

She looked me over with interest. To state the obvious, there can be no reaction if there is no action. Just a matter of cause and effect. Yet, for some reason, it felt like she was curiously observing a static object about to move on its own.

"Did you want to talk about something?" I asked.

"Oh, yeah. It's about Maori Hino... Are you two really dating?"

I floundered. I'd guessed she was going to ask me something like that, but the words still stuck in my throat.

"I guess so," I managed to say. She looked surprised.

"So it's true. But it's so out of the blue. You didn't even know her, right?"

"The heart is a mysterious thing."

"You mean it was love at first sight?"

"Um, yeah. I guess," I said vaguely. Wataya looked like she was deep in thought.

"It's going to sound bad to say this with no context, but...," she began.

"Say what?"

"Just that...if you don't really like her, and you just said it to mess around or on an impulse, I wish you'd take it back."

I looked at her, caught off guard. Did she know something? Only a couple of guys in my class had overheard my conversation with Hino, and I doubted they'd make a big deal of it on social media or anything.

"Why do you think I don't like her?" I asked, setting my other question aside for the moment. She furrowed her eyebrows slightly.

"Well, I have a reputation for being cold and blunt, and it's pretty accurate, but Maori is important to me. If I can protect her from being hurt, I will. I started looking for you as soon as I heard what happened, because it just doesn't seem like you like her."

She'd seen through me. I didn't know what to say.

"How would you know that?" I managed to ask.

"I just do. You're like me. You even talk in a cold way. Normally, if someone asked you about a girl you fell for at first sight, you'd show some emotion on your face. But you didn't even look embarrassed. You just looked annoyed."

I stared at her. Was something showing on my face right now, too? Should I tell her I'd lied about liking Hino?

And finally, you can't fall in love with me.

I remembered Hino's words. She seemed to have figured out right away that I wasn't being sincere, that there was something else to it. Maybe that was why she'd gone along with it, and Wataya might not know about the conditions.

"Anyway, I'm meeting her after school. Can we talk another time?" I said, trying to dodge the issue.

Wataya gave me a long look. Her expression didn't change, and I couldn't tell what she was thinking. Her eyes darted away for a moment.

"Sorry. I know how weird all of this must sound to you. It's also awkward of me to bring it up as soon as we meet. You don't seem like a bad guy. I don't think you'll hurt her. Sorry. I just wanted to talk to you a little."

I made a poor attempt at a fake smile.

"Uh, okay. So you accomplished your goal?"

"Basically. Oh, one more thing. If you ever run into trouble with her, you can talk to me. Can we at least exchange contact info?"

I had an old flip phone, so I opted to exchange email addresses. After that, Wataya left. I wanted to talk to Hino right away, but I remembered the first condition (don't talk to each other until after school), so I went back to my classroom.

When I sat down, Shimokawa asked curiously, "Did you have to talk to Wataya about something?"

"Hard to say. Kind of yes, kind of no," I said noncommittally. Shimokawa looked down.

"I feel like I caused you trouble again."

"No, no way. Why?"

"I mean…they haven't done anything today. And while I was out yesterday, your life changed drastically. You said you told Hino that you liked her. I feel like they forced you to do something because of me."

There was something childlike about his earnestness. Shimokawa got teased for being slightly pudgy, but he's got a beautiful heart. You can't see a person's heart, though. Heartless people made fun of him and took out their anger on him. That's what led to the bullying. I pushed back, so they started targeting me. People stopped talking to me, which made Shimokawa worried, so he started reaching out to me on a regular basis.

I don't care about being isolated or being bullied in that immature manner. That should have been a good thing, but since I completely ignored the bullies, they went back to bothering Shimokawa in a crueler and meaner way. I hadn't realized it right away, but they even started taking his money. When Shimokawa stayed home from school, I confronted the bullies, and that's when I struck the deal with the ringleader. That was how I ended up telling Hino I liked her.

I felt bad about doing that to her, but I figured she would just reject me and brush it off, and later I could give her my sincere apology. Though, everything went off the rails, including my answer to her.

Swearing Shimokawa to secrecy, I told him everything that had happened except her three conditions for dating me. At first, he had on a blank expression as he listened, but at a certain point, he started looking unsettled, and finally, surprised.

"So that's what happened," he said when I was done.

"Yeah. I figure I'll talk to her about it after school."

"Well, thanks. You've come to my rescue again. But…"

He paused, looking anxious.

"What?"

"Nothing, it's just… I'm not sure they're the kind of people who will give up that easily. I'm changing schools, and once I'm gone, I'm worried they'll harass you again."

Shimokawa was suddenly moving to China. I hoped it didn't have to do with the bullying, but he said it was because of his parents' situation. Summer vacation starts earlier in China than Japan and in mid-June in some places. They timed their move with that in mind and were tying up all the loose ends in preparation.

"I'll deal with that when it happens. You don't need to worry about it. You've only got two weeks left here. We should try to enjoy it," I said.

He still seemed worried, but he nodded and said, "Okay." Then he smiled, which I hadn't seen him do at school for a long time.

The rest of the day passed peacefully, and the bullies left us alone. But my meeting with Hino was hanging over my head. We hadn't decided where to meet. I wasn't sure what to do, but I'd mentioned which class I was in the day before, so I decided to wait in my classroom. When homeroom was over, I said goodbye to Shimokawa.

Neither of us were in a club or on a sports team, so we always walked to the station together. I was worried the bullies would try to take his money or something if he was walking by himself, but he said his mom was coming to school to turn in some paperwork related to their move; they would talk to our teacher and then drive home.

I scanned the classroom from my seat by the window. The bullies were gone. I took a magazine out of my bag and sat at my desk, killing time. As the classroom emptied out, I could hear the school band tuning their instruments and the sports teams warming up in the distance. I sort of liked that feeling of being halfway between isolation and group solidarity. The blue sky outside the square window panel made the empty classroom feel like something from a sad song.

I'm not sure how long I sat there like that. The sounds from other classes had gone silent, and the hallway outside the open door was empty.

Then I heard footsteps approaching. They weren't hurried, but they weren't relaxed, either. They sounded like the footsteps of someone heading straight toward their destination with a hint of nervousness.

The footsteps stopped. I looked toward the door. *She* was standing there. She raised her eyebrows briefly in surprise, then smiled innocently.

"Found my boyfriend! Tooru Kamiya, right?"

It was none other than Maori Hino herself.

"Uh, yeah." I nodded.

She looked at me with deep interest. All things considered, she'd sounded so casual a second earlier. I'd been prepared for the worst. As I was thinking about that, she walked into the classroom.

"Mind if I sit here?" she asked, walking straight to the seat in front of me, sitting sideways in it. Her black hair shimmered centimeters from my eyes. She repositioned herself so she was facing me. When our eyes met, she smiled happily.

"Aren't you in a club?" she asked before I could say anything.

"Me? No. Are you?"

She set her elbow on the desk and rested her chin in her palm. She was grinning. I'd never seen someone look so happy in that pose.

"I'm not in anything, either. The go-home club, as they say. I'm glad you're not busy with anything. I didn't ask yesterday, and I was worried you might have skipped today because of me."

I didn't see a lot of smiles in my everyday life. I made the daily round of school, home, and supermarket. Dad and I don't smile much, either. Hino, on the other hand, wore all sorts of facial expressions. She took her hand from her chin.

"Also, sorry for not saying where we should meet after school. I was so relieved when I saw you sitting here. I have a lot of things to ask you about dating."

"Yes, about that…," I said, looking away. Out of the corner of my eye, I saw her tense up slightly.

"Changed your mind?" she asked. "I thought you might, since I laid out all those weird conditions. Guess it's unavoidable. How sad. I'm sorry to pull you into this awkward situation."

"Oh, no, not at all," I responded, trying to decide what to do. Should I tell her the truth and take back what I'd said?

"Wataya came here after second period," I said, trying to hide my confusion.

"Yeah, I heard," she said. "Since she was there when you came up to me yesterday, I told her what happened. She took an interest, I guess. Anyway…sorry about that. I didn't tell anyone else, but no one likes being talked about."

She lowered her voice, looking guilty. I hadn't meant to make her feel that way.

"No, it's fine," I said hurriedly. "It's normal to tell stuff like that to your friends. So you two are close?"

"Yeah. Izumi looks normal, but she's actually pretty weird. Just when you're thinking how oddly calm she is, she'll say something super bizarre. It's so funny. And she's a really good person, so I always end up telling her everything."

So Wataya's first name was Izumi. Mulling this discovery, I said, "I could kind of tell that from talking to her. But about what I said yesterday…"

This time, I went through with it. I gave her the backstory. I thought she'd be upset, but she didn't seem very surprised, and she even smiled happily when I finished.

"Oh, so that's what happened. I thought it was some sort of dare, but you did it to help someone getting bullied. Very impressive!"

"It wasn't a big deal. He's a good guy, considering he's willing to be friends with someone like me. I didn't want him to have a rough time. He's switching schools soon, actually."

"Really? That's too bad."

"Yeah. Anyway…I know I said yes to your conditions. It's weird. I don't know why I did."

I noticed she was staring at me.

"Tooru, do you not want to date me?"

It had been a long time since anyone but my dad called me by my first name. Strangely enough, the simple act of her saying my name made it seem more special somehow.

"I don't know… Maybe."

"What's that supposed to mean?" she asked, smirking like she found this entertaining.

I tried to smile but failed, instead searching for something to say.

"This might sound rude, but I thought it might be kind of fun," I said. "Three conditions, right? We wouldn't really be what people normally call boyfriend and girlfriend, would we? More like a fake couple. We're not allowed to fall in love, so if you're okay with it, I guess I am, too," I finally concluded. She rested her elbow on my desk again and rested her chin in it, smiling her happy smile.

"Then let's do it! But Izumi will worry, so we'll have to tell everyone we're dating for real. I didn't tell her about my conditions."

That was the odd agreement we came to that day. We were going to date, with certain rules in place.

3

"I'm home! Hey, that smells great."

I heard the front door open as I was cooking curry for dinner. A minute later, Dad poked his head into the kitchen.

"The usual Wednesday-night curry," I said. "By the way, Dad, I'm seeing someone now. I thought I should tell you."

"What?" Dad said, widening his eyes in response to my dutiful announcement. At my sister's suggestion, we had all agreed to tell each other important things when they happened.

"Seeing someone… You mean a girlfriend?"

"I guess dating a boy is a possibility, but yes, a girlfriend."

"That's not what I meant. I mean, it is, but—it's just so sudden," Dad said, sitting down at the table still in his work clothes. I always ask him to put his work clothes in the laundry when he comes home, but he can't shake the habit. Considering he's the one who pays the bills, though, I don't push too hard.

"So you've reached that age," he mumbled emotionally.

"It's not like anything's going to change. I just wanted to tell you," I answered.

The day before, after we decided to date, Hino and I had sat and talked for a long time.

"So, do you mind if I ask you some questions?" she inquired.

I shook my head to show her it was fine. She took out her phone to take notes and basically started interviewing me.

"When's your birthday?"

"February twenty-fifth."

"Got it, February twenty-fifth. Hey, that's Renoir's birthday!"

"I had no idea. Is it really?"

"Yup. Can I ask about your family?"

"I live with my dad, just the two of us."

"I see."

"Why do you look like you just figured something out?"

"Because you seem to have your things together for someone our age."

"Do I? When I was in my last year of junior high, I came to school with a rubber band around my wrist, and after that everyone started calling me Mum."

"I love it. A junior high kid whose nickname is Mum."

"You're writing that down?"

"I am. Blood type?"

"AB."

"Makes sense."

"And? What about you?"

"…AB."

"Makes sense."

"You're making fun of me."

"I am not. Any more questions?"

"Who do you respect?"

"…Keiko Nishikawa."

"I'm sorry, but who is that?"

"A geeky author of literary fiction."

"What do you like about her?"

"She's very sanitary."

"…Sanitary? Do you mean clean?"

"You can fake being clean, but I don't think you can fake being sanitary."

"You're an interesting guy."

She asked me a bunch more questions, about my hobbies, the celebrities I like, movies, places, whether I like cats or dogs, what I do on my days off, my favorite foods, et cetera, et cetera.

I asked a few of the same questions back, and she answered most of them. She likes dogs and parks, apparently, and she's crazy for sweets. She seemed like the typical girl.

It was still daylight, but the moon was already visible. For whatever reason, she said, "Let's do something people who are dating would do."

According to her, that would be to take a picture on their phones. It turned out funny. Against the orange background of the classroom, she was cheerfully making a peace sign while I made an awkward, embarrassed face.

I told her I had a flip phone, and we exchanged numbers. She sent me the photo and suggested I use it for my home screen, but that was more than I could stomach. Afterward, we walked to the station together, since we both commute by train. She scampered around, chasing her shadow.

We discovered that we took the same train line, and in the same direction, too. I took it three stops, and she took it four. We decided to take the train together after school as often as possible.

We weren't on the train for very long, but talking while sitting next to her gave me a sort of indescribable feeling of restlessness.

I didn't go into that much detail with my dad and just gave him the basic story over dinner. Since Hino had asked me to keep the fact that we weren't genuinely dating a secret, I kept that to myself.

After he'd finished all his curry and rice, Dad sat in front of his empty plate and closed his eyes. He made an unintelligible noise of appreciation, then abruptly got up and went to his room, which is next to the living room.

Our house isn't very big, but Dad had managed to make enough space for a simple family altar. He sat down in front of it and started talking to Mom.

"Tooru has a girlfriend now. I was worried about him because he never talked about girls, so this is a relief."

"Please, Dad, would you stop saying weird stuff to Mom?" I pleaded.

"It's not weird stuff. I think you having a girlfriend is something I ought to tell your mother. If Sanae were here, I'm sure… Well…"

He let my sister's name slip, but as soon as he said it, he seemed lost. I think he feels guilty. He doesn't say it, but I know he believes she left because she was ashamed of him.

"Stop babbling and help me clean up dinner for once, would you?" I said.

"Oh, right. Of course."

After dinner, we always do our own thing.

I finished washing the dishes and was folding the laundry and ironing handkerchiefs and uniforms when Dad came out from the bath. I took my turn before the water got cold.

My sister didn't leave because she was disgusted with Dad. Even though we usually share everything with each other, something happened that she couldn't tell him. That was why she left.

I finished showering and got in the tub. It's too small for me to stretch my legs out, but it was a place where I could relieve all my tension.

A lot of stuff had happened that day. The next day would probably be the same.

I used to think I'd never surprise myself. However, just the day before, I'd answered yes to Hino's proposition. I never thought I could do something like that… I wondered what Sanae would say if I told her

I was dating someone. I smiled wryly at the thought and got out of the bath. After drying off, I put on my boxers. I glanced in the mirror.

There was my slightly gaunt self, looking nervous as usual.

4

My daily routine didn't change that much after I got a girlfriend.

The next day, I went to school like normal. On the train, on the walk to school, and at the school entrance, I caught myself looking for Hino and Wataya. That was a different feeling. A new person had come into my life.

In class, I talked to Shimokawa. He was moving next weekend. We hadn't been friends for long, but it was sad for someone to be leaving my life, just as Hino was coming into it. Although I should have been used to that by now.

"Can I ask you something?" Shimokawa said.

He always asked for my advice about various things. Today it was about his weight.

"You think I should try to lose a few?"

This was the third time we'd talked about it. I told him no, like I always did.

"Think about it, Shimokawa. Commoners don't have the luxury of having flab."

"But I hear that in the US, people think you can't control yourself if you're overweight."

"Maybe, but what Americans consider fat is totally different from what Japanese consider fat. I don't think they would even classify you as overweight."

Shimokawa gazed at his stomach.

"I'll root for you if you want to diet, but don't you think it's bad to push yourself too hard?"

"I dunno."

"Also, there's the view that some people don't look right without a few extra pounds on them."

"What do you mean?"

"I could easily eat a kilo of steak out of affection for you. With a second helping."

"You're insane."

"You, fat? Where? In my eyes, you're a slender lady."

"And you're an insane knight in shining armor."

"I pledge to you that I will never leave a scrap of food on my plate, maybe not until my deathbed, but at least from the first to the last bite of my meal."

"It doesn't make sense, but I love it. Maybe I'll just be a crazy fat guy."

I definitely was not messing with him, but he always tended to over-think things and get depressed. To prevent that, I tried to keep the conversation as upbeat as possible.

He looked pleased with himself for a while after that and started thinking of pickup lines you could only make if you're fat. Then he remembered he never talked to girls and ended up sitting in front of his highly nourishing bento, looking at the ceiling.

"Kamiya, I always learn a lot from you, but in the end, it all comes down to the importance of taking action."

"Huh? Is something wrong?" I asked, pausing as I opened my own bento. I wondered if I'd inadvertently hurt his feelings earlier. But he didn't look upset.

"No. But now that I'm about to change schools, I'm realizing a lot of things. You've always tried to cheer me up. I've been lucky to know you. I wish I'd made the effort to make friends with some girls, too."

Even though he was expressing regrets, he sounded okay about the situation. I couldn't help smiling.

"You should get to know the girls at your next school. It'll be a brand-new place, and you have the chance to be a new person."

"If I have any luck, I'll introduce some of them to you. Oh, but Hino might get mad."

He didn't know we weren't a real couple.

I smiled back noncommittally.

After school, I waited for Hino in my classroom again. As Shimo-kawa left, he called out, "See you tomorrow." It was so natural, I answered without thinking. But as I flipped through my magazine, I realized something.

He was by himself today. I immediately closed it and exited the classroom.

Afraid the bullies might go after him again, I ran to the shoe lockers near the front entrance. His indoor shoes were there, and his outdoor shoes were gone. That seemed like strong evidence they hadn't pulled him into a bathroom somewhere inside school or anything. Still, I was worried, so I quickly changed my shoes and went outside. I saw him strolling toward the front gate.

I let out a sigh of relief. There was no sign of anyone lurking in the shadows to drag him off. As I stood there, I heard someone behind me.

"What's the big rush?"

I knew who it was from the voice. I turned around, and there he was—the ringleader. The same person who made me tell Hino I liked her.

"You're that worried about fatso?"

"Of course I am. He's my friend," I snapped. He smiled mockingly.

"Your friend, huh?"

He gave me a long look, then told me that today at lunch, our homeroom teacher and the guidance counselor had given him a warning about Shimokawa. This was news to me.

"The asshole recorded us hassling him for money."

"Recorded you? Shimokawa did?"

"Yeah, the second or third time we did it."

His voice was dry with resignation, like he was talking about someone else.

"I never expected a spineless, passive lump like him to pull that shit. What a joke. And you know what he said when the counselor asked why he did it so late in the game? He said he didn't care what happened to him, but he was worried that after he left, we might take money from you or from other students, so he made up his mind to snitch on us."

According to him, when Shimokawa's mom came to school the previous day to fill out the transfer paperwork, Shimokawa stayed afterward to talk to the homeroom teacher and counselor.

I could hardly speak from shock. Shimokawa cared that much about me?

"You should have known this would happen eventually if you kept pulling stunts like that," I said. "Why? Why did you do it? You must have worked hard to get into this school."

He smirked but looked somewhat dejected.

"Good question... I'm not sure. I thought I was a decent student, but at some point, I started skipping class like it was no big deal. The kids I thought were my friends, they turned on me, said I told them what to do. Since money's involved, Shimokawa's parents showed up saying I better apologize before they go to the police. I guess Shimokawa said he didn't need the money back, but they asked for it anyway."

He sniggered again, then let out a moan.

"Why does my life suck all of a sudden? Why do you think, Kamiya?"

I didn't know what to say, so I just stared at him. With a sneer, he started walking toward the gate. Was he going to chase after Shimokawa? Would he attack him in desperation? No, he probably wasn't that much of an idiot. He'd worked hard and had enough ambition to get into this school to start with. He'd just taken a few wrong turns...

I went back to the classroom. Everyone was gone. I sat down at my desk and took out my phone, which I hardly ever use. I was going to call Shimokawa, but I stopped just before I pressed the call button. He had his own plans. I should probably pretend I didn't know anything until he brought it up. I took out my magazine and started reading. Like the day before, Hino suddenly showed up.

"Ah, there he is. Found my boyfriend," she called from the doorway. I was kind of relieved to see her, even though I hardly knew her. It felt strange that there was a girl who wanted to come see me.

"What am I supposed to say to that?" I asked with a wry smile. She thought for a minute.

"'Hi, honey,' or something?"

"I feel like people don't even say that in foreign movies anymore."

"Aha, so my boyfriend doesn't like to call his girlfriend *honey*."

"You're writing that down?"

While she was typing on her phone, someone said in an exasperated voice, "Oh, come on, you two, enough with the flirting, please."

Wataya peered in from the hallway. She looked as if she had heartburn from eating something too sweet. I'd seen her with Hino a couple of times, but the three of us had never talked together like this before.

"So you're hanging out with us today?" I asked.

"I was worried about you two," she said, stepping into the classroom and walking toward my desk. Hino followed, gazing intently at me.

"What?" I stared back at her.

"Oh, nothing. Nothing at all," she responded, and laughed.

"Anyway, Kamiya, don't you think you should be happy that two beautiful ladies came to see you?"

Talking with her the previous day, I had gotten the sense that Wataya was a little unapproachable and very straightforward.

"Haven't you ever heard that guys get used to even beautiful women after three days, Wataya?" I teased. She must not have been expecting that, because she looked impressed and smiled.

"I believe the saying is 'guys get bored of even beautiful women after three days.' And anyway, we haven't known each other for three days yet. You only had a proper conversation with Maori for the first time yesterday, right?"

"That's right," Maori answered cheerfully. "We got to know each other yesterday."

"And what did you learn?"

Hino told Wataya the basic facts about my life, except the stuff regarding my family, maybe because she was being discreet about the single-parent thing. Wataya said her blood type was AB, too.

"I feel like this is a gathering of three weirdos," she declared happily.

"But, Izumi, don't they say three heads are better than two?" Maori asked.

"With our three heads, we're more like a chimera," she shot back. I could tell they were close friends from their banter. Hino was perpetually cheerful while Wataya stayed cool.

"Anyway, Tooru mentioned he likes the author Keiko Nishikawa."

Wataya looked surprised.

"Keiko Nishikawa? That's an odd choice. But I noticed you were reading *Literary World*. What are you, a bookworm?" she asked, and started spouting her own opinions about the magazine.

Literary World is one of the main magazines covering literary fiction in Japan. Some stories they've published by new writers have been nominated for the super-famous Akutagawa Prize. Keiko Nishikawa has published some stuff in *Literary World*, but I never expected someone in my grade to know who she is or even know about the magazine.

"No, I'm not really a bookworm," I answered. "But how do you know about Keiko Nishikawa and this magazine, Wataya?"

I don't get an allowance, but one of my pleasures is buying magazines and books with the money left over from being thrifty with our household budget. Dad reads them, too, so we split the cost.

"Oh, I love literary fiction," Wataya answered nonchalantly. "I like

French and Japanese movies, too, and lately I've gotten into Russian films. The quirky, gloomy ones that obviously aren't trying to win over the masses."

Again, I was amazed to hear these things coming from the mouth of a girl my age. Out of the corner of my eye, I saw Hino writing something on her phone.

"Hino, you better not be writing down that I'm a bookworm."

"You're not? Okay. I'll write that you're a bookworm who doesn't like to be called one."

"I feel like I'm shooting myself in the foot here."

The three of us decided to spend the afternoon together and headed toward the station. Wataya and I were walking next to each other, talking about books and authors, when I heard a shutter sound behind me and turned around.

"Hino, why are you taking our picture?" I asked.

She was using her phone to photograph Wataya and me. She flashed me a look like an elementary school kid caught misbehaving.

"Don't be rude, Kamiya. Does a girl need a reason to take a picture of her boyfriend?" Wataya asked pointedly. She didn't know we weren't really boyfriend and girlfriend.

"I guess not. I'm just not used to it."

"Well, get used to it. It's already the third day since you guys started dating."

"Don't be ridiculous. I'm not even used to talking to two beautiful women yet."

"I thought you said you were used to us earlier."

"But three full days haven't passed yet."

As we were rehashing our conversation from the classroom, Hino interrupted.

"So, guys. In order to get used to each other, how about we go get something to drink and deepen our relationship?"

"A café? I guess that's fine," I answered.

We started talking about where to go, but the family restaurants and cafés they suggested were all out of my price range. I don't carry a lot of extra cash with me.

"Don't worry about it," Wataya said. "I'm tagging along stealing your alone time, so the least I can do is cover you. Besides, I have a job, even though we're not supposed to, so I have some spending money."

"But I don't really like other people paying for me," I said.

"Seriously, it's not a big deal."

Hino, who had been lost in thought while I wrangled with Wataya, suddenly spoke up.

"Better yet, how about we go to Tooru's house? Then we won't have to spend any money."

"Wuh…?"

Naturally, I was the one who sounded like there was no brain in between my ears.

5

Ultimately, I convinced myself it would be okay because Wataya was with us, so we all went to my house. Which is to say, my little apartment in a housing development that has nothing whatsoever prideworthy about it.

"Wow, your house is so clean!" Hino exclaimed, peering around curiously. "Can I take a picture?"

"Uh, I guess so."

No female had stepped foot in our house since my sister left. I felt like my usual drab surroundings had just gotten a tiny bit brighter. It didn't feel real. I couldn't believe we had ended up here.

I asked the two of them to sit at the dining table while I put on some water for black tea. My dad and I drink black tea three days a week, so I knew how to brew it quite well. Meanwhile, Hino and Wataya were chatting in the way that girls usually talk with each other.

"Kamiya's house is seriously neat and tidy," Wataya was saying. "No one's here right now, but is his mom a neat freak or something?"

"Ah, I didn't tell you this earlier, but it's just my dad and me. Cleaning is kind of my hobby. I keep up with it pretty well," I said simply as I watched the timer for the tea bags.

"Oh yes," Hino said proudly. "Being sanitary is very important to my boyfriend."

"Being sanitary? Not being clean?" Wataya asked, skipping over the bit about me having a single parent.

"Nope. You can fake being clean, but you can't fake being sanitary. Take a good look at Tooru's shirt. The collar and sleeves are perfectly wrinkle-free. And he washes and irons his handkerchief every day. Keeping the things no one sees clean is a sign of good sanitation."

"Wow," Wataya said, sounding impressed. "I didn't realize till we talked, but you're a strange one, Kamiya."

"Like you're not?" I retorted. "Also, tea's ready!"

I dumped out the hot water I'd poured into the teacups to warm them up and poured the Lady Grey tea from the ceramic teapot. The distinctive citrusy scent of bergamot filled the kitchen.

"Please accept this humble brew," I said.

"We're not having green tea, are we?" Wataya said.

"Oh right, you don't say that when you serve black tea," I answered, bringing their cups to the table. Then I brought my own cup along with a white plate with cookies piled on top that I'd bought on sale.

We still have three chairs from when my sister lived with us. I sat down and sipped my tea. The orange-and-lemon-scented tea went down easy, soothing my nerves.

"This is so good! Tooru, you make a good cuppa. And it smells amazing," said Hino, who was sitting across from me. She looked surprised.

"…Oh wow, it does. What is this? What brand?"

Apparently Wataya liked it, too. I sighed secretly with relief.

"Just a cheap supermarket brand. Lady Grey is inexpensive and good. But I steeped it a tiny bit too long. I'd give myself a seven out of ten. Anyone want some more? There's plenty," I said before going to get the still-full teapot.

I pulled a fluffy tea cozy stuffed with cotton batting over the pot and set it on the table. My sister taught me how to sew, so making a tea cozy was easy. As I sipped my tea, I noticed the two of them staring at me.

"What?" I asked.

"I didn't notice it before, but you're like some kind of downfallen aristocrat. Like, you're oddly refined."

"Don't call me downfallen. And, Hino, don't write that down!"

We chatted about various things until the pot and the plate were empty. Eventually, the two of them started poking around the house, but there wasn't much to see, considering it's an old, boring two-bedroom apartment. I wasn't about to show them Dad's room, so the only things to see were the living room and my room. Wataya looked at my bookshelf for a long time while Hino took a bunch of pictures. Whatever. That's fine.

"Hino, why do you like taking pictures so much?" I asked. "There's nothing interesting to photograph here."

"That's not true," she answered. "I've never actually been in a guy's room before. It's very interesting!"

Just then, with the voice of some strange old man none of us knew, Wataya made a remark.

"My oh my, Kamiya. You have excellent taste. These rare books would be worth a fortune if you sold them to an antique book dealer. Where'd you get them?"

"My dad hunted for these ones at used bookstores. He's the type who buys books and leaves them lying all over, so I end up putting them on shelves in the living room or my room."

They both made vague sounds like maybe they were impressed, maybe not.

"You're really on top of things, Tooru. All these books and your room isn't even dusty."

"What can I say? Sanitation is important."

"Sanitation again!"

"Please, Wataya, you sound like a cockroach."

After that, for some reason, they both said they wanted to see me iron, so I took down the laundry, stashed my underwear away, and ironed some handkerchiefs and shirts. Wataya said I was so good, it was intimidating, and Hino took a video.

Around sunset, I walked them to the station. I figured I'd do the evening shopping at the same time, so I grabbed a reusable shopping bag I'd gotten as a free gift.

"Oh wow, that bag suits the downfallen aristocrat perfectly. Honestly, are you even a high school student?"

Hino snapped a picture of Wataya suppressing a smile.

The whole day felt unreal.

That night, after I finished preparing dinner, I was sitting at the table reviewing my textbooks when I heard the door open. Dad was home. He was late, and when he poked his head into the kitchen, his face was flushed. He seemed to have stopped somewhere to drink again, even though he can't hold his liquor.

"Dad, if you're going to go out for drinks after work, at least let me know."

"Sorry, I couldn't help myself. I was so happy to hear you have a girlfriend."

When I told him my girlfriend and her friend had come over to hang out earlier, he gaped in surprise.

"You brought them here?"

"I didn't show them your room or anything. I thought it would be okay with you."

"Of course it is. But I think... Doesn't it smell good in here?"

"Please, Dad, promise me you'll never say weird things like that in public."

I sighed and walked into the kitchen to warm his dinner up. Dad sat down in a kitchen chair and stared at me.

"What?"

"You went and grew up on me."

I didn't say anything as I took the stew out of the fridge. Dad poured himself another glass, even though I'd asked him before not to drink at home. He nibbled at the dinner I'd made while he sipped at his low-malt beer. He was passed out before it was half-empty.

"Dammit, he hasn't even taken a bath."

I dampened a towel with warm water, woke him up, and told him to at least wipe himself down with it. While he was doing that, I went to his room and laid out his futon. Another time, he'd fallen asleep on the sofa and was sore the next day. As I was squatting down to fix his futon, the man of the house came staggering in.

"Are you okay? You know you can't hold your alcohol, so you should take it easy. Hey, at least change out of your work clothes!"

"Don't worry, Sanae. I'm fine."

I froze, and he didn't notice. He changed into his pajamas and lay down on the futon. I looked at him. He must have been really drunk, because he'd just mistaken me for my sister.

6

"My house is kind of like yours, so I'm sure you'll feel at home," Wataya said.

It was the next day after school, and we'd decided to go to her house, partly because it was close enough for me to use my commuter pass to get there.

School that day had been uneventful. Shimokawa seemed relaxed, and the main bully was by himself, separated from his group of friends. I saw him looking at a magazine with job listings, but I didn't talk to him. After school, I met up with the girls, and the three of us headed to Wataya's house. She took the train as well. She was on the same line as Hino and me but only two stops away from school.

She lived in an apartment building with an automated lock on the front entrance. I gazed at the fancy entryway with longing. I'd always wished we had a similar lock for our building.

"Another picture, Hino?"

She turned to me and held up her phone, smiling.

"I wanted a video of my boyfriend in awe."

"Looking stupid is more like it. You shouldn't waste your phone storage like that."

"It's no big deal."

"Stop flirting and come inside!" Wataya shouted.

We followed her to the elevator hall. She told us she lived with her mom, who designed book jackets. Her mom worked at night, but during the day, she was often out running errands, apparently. Sometimes, as a part-time job, Wataya helped her by looking for reference materials, writing up documents, and organizing receipts. Her father lived separately for reasons she didn't go into. To be honest, I felt kind of nervous about visiting a house inhabited only by women.

"So, guys, sit down!"

Their apartment was significantly larger than mine. She led us to the spacious living room, which had a lot of pictures on the walls and carefully chosen furniture and decorations, like you'd expect a designer to have in their house. They were on the top floor of a ten-story building, with soaring views of the sky, and the laundry was—

"Sorry, Wataya, I just saw something I shouldn't have."

"Huh? Oh, that. No worries. I don't care, but it probably bothers you. Sorry about that."

Hino and I sat across from each other in the living room and waited while Wataya prepared tea for us. I noticed Hino staring at me again.

"What's wrong, Hino?"

"Downfallen aristocrat."

"I told you to forget about that!"

"Sorry. It just fits you so well."

She might have been praising me in her own way, but I wasn't exactly overjoyed by the nickname. It must have shown on my face, because she said, "Don't make that face. You should smile more."

"I didn't think I was making a weird expression," I said, but I knew I probably was.

In contrast, she was grinning cheerfully as usual.

"You're always smiling," I mumbled unenthusiastically. She raised her eyebrows.

"Yeah, I know. Well, not always. I try to when I can. Because when you can't smile, you just can't…"

I couldn't help staring at her. As soon as she noticed my surprised expression, she started walking it back.

"Oh, I'm not talking from personal experience. Just some stuff I read in a manga."

"Really?" I asked suspiciously. She nodded with a grin I could tell was fake.

"Really."

"Okay, but still…," I said, leaning toward her and lowering my voice so Wataya wouldn't overhear us. "We might be a fake couple, but if something's wrong, I hope you'll tell me."

"What?… Oh, right."

I looked at her surprised face from close up. Just then, Wataya came in holding a tray.

"If you're going to flirt, can you at least do it where I can't see you?" she said.

Hino answered with a joke, like she always did.

"But, Izumi, you might still hear us."

"Oooh, an adult joke. You're very confident now that you have a boyfriend."

She set the tray down on the table and started tickling Hino. She resisted but eventually broke out laughing. I watched them, but my mind was on Hino's words.

Because when you can't smile, you just can't.

She said she was talking about a manga she read, but it sounded like she was speaking from experience. Or was I misreading her? I watched her playing around with Wataya. You can't see a person's heart; you can't look inside. Her smile seemed carefree and happy.

7

The days passed quietly. Hino and I have been dating for more than a week. The only major change was the way I spent my time after school.

Or was it?

Lately, Hino seemed to be all I thought about. I'd remember her smiling with her chin in her hand, and her beautiful, healthy hair that seemed alive to the very ends. When it caught the evening sun, it shone like silk. Was I only captivated by her appearance? Was I misinterpreting my feelings because I'd had so little interaction with girls before now?

I felt like there was more to it.

I couldn't stop thinking about what she'd said that one afternoon. I wanted to know what she was hiding behind her perpetual smile. If I could, I wanted to help her. Those thoughts would engulf my mind when I least expected it.

"Kamiya, your mind seems like it's somewhere else lately," Shimokawa said one day at lunch in the middle of our conversation.

"Really? I don't think that's true," I said with a smile, glossing it over. Shimokawa had on a gentle expression.

"Oh, by the way, you know how I asked you about books a while ago? I've been ordering Japanese novels and stockpiling them. They won't be easy to get once I'm in China."

I was slightly confused by the sudden change of topic, but I remembered that conversation.

"You did say something about that. Did you find any good ones?"

"Yeah, lots of great stuff, but my favorite is the collection of proverbs. You can find them online, but somehow a book feels sturdier, like this body of mine."

He thumped his stomach. He probably brought the topic up to make me smile, and I fell right into his trap.

"You'll be like a walking dictionary of proverbs."

"Anyone can walk, but taking the first step is never easy."

"I've never heard that proverb. Who said it?"

"Shimokawa, the big eater. Brief biography: did nothing much during his life."

He got me with that one. I chuckled. I was starting to genuinely enjoy the conversation. I told him I'd heard smart guys got all the girls overseas. He looked happy about that.

"By the way, do you know a proverb that goes 'you can't hide a cough' and something?" he asked.

"Hmm…," I started, then hesitated. We had a collection of proverbs at home that I'd read. The one he'd mentioned was under the "Love" category.

You can't hide love or coughs.

"Wasn't it 'you can't hide sneezes or coughs'?" I said, playing innocent.

"That's it!" he said with a smile.

That was how my days passed. At school, I talked to Shimokawa as usual, and afterward, I hung out with Hino. I'm not used to sending texts and am not especially good at it, so I didn't stay in touch with her all the time. When I apologized for it, she just told me not to worry.

"Anyway, you're following the second condition," she added.

Instead, we had long conversations after school in my classroom.

"So you do all the cooking? I'm sure you're a way better cook than me," she said one day.

"I don't know if I'm good at it, but I manage."

"That's a verbal tic of my boyfriend's. 'I manage.'"

"Are you writing that down on your phone? Anyway, I don't have a habit of saying that."

I hadn't had any serious conversations with Hino since the day at Wataya's house. Maybe I could have forced it out of her, but I didn't want to do that.

We were a couple and not a couple. One of the conditions of our relationship was that we couldn't fall in love. At first, it was easy. I was the one who started the whole thing. I didn't know her reasons, but being in a fake relationship didn't bother me.

Maybe faking it made it real, or maybe there is no such thing as real love. Either way, I was puzzled by the way that dating Hino steadily changed me.

It was the second Friday since we started seeing each other. The next day was a day off.

"Hino, I was wondering about this weekend. It's June now. How about we go somewhere?"

"I can't believe it's June already!"

Her face clouded over slightly. But just as quickly, she smiled and said, "I'm sorry! You wanted to talk about the weekend. Do you have any plans?"

"Sunday, my friend Shimokawa is moving, so I'm going to see him off."

I'd told her about him before, and I'd wanted to introduce them, but Shimokawa had rejected the idea. When I asked why, he said that having more friends would only make it harder to leave.

"Make the most of your time with her," he'd said. "I've gotten to hang out with you a lot."

He smiled calmly, and I realized he was one of the few close friends I had. He was moving overseas, but it wasn't like we were saying good-bye for eternity. There were plenty of ways to stay in contact. We could still remain friends. It made me sad to think about him leaving, but at the moment, I focused on my conversation with Hino.

"I'm free all day Saturday, though," I continued. "Where should we go?"

Hino looked caught off guard.

"You mean…we're going on a date?"

"I guess so. We don't have to if you don't want to. I was just wondering what we should do on the weekends. You were probably busy last Saturday."

"Yeah. I had a doctor's appointment. Nothing serious."

She glanced away for a moment. I might not have noticed a week ago.

"But a date sounds fun. Let's do it! I'm not free until the afternoon, though. Is that okay?"

Distracted by her initial reaction, I was slow to respond.

"Huh? Oh, sure. Are you always busy in the morning on weekends? According to the rules, we're not supposed to talk to each other until after school, but how about other days?" I asked, boldly bringing up the point that had been bothering me.

"Girl stuff," she said, shying away from a real answer. "Anyway, what should we do? Where should we go? I bet you usually spend the weekend reading and doing chores."

When she put it that way, it sounded pretty dull.

"Yeah, basically," I answered.

"And we should try not to spend too much money, right?"

"Unfortunately, yes," I said, bowing my head.

"No worries!" she said in a hurry. "How about we go to the park? If you don't mind, you could make us bentos, and in exchange, I'll treat us to dessert at a café afterward. That would be doable, right?"

I was grateful for the suggestion. Financially and emotionally.

"Definitely. Any particular requests for your lunch?"

"I eat everything, so all challengers are welcome. Oh, but I'd like to have some of that tea you made!"

"Got it. All challengers, huh? I noticed this before, but sometimes your choice of words really baffles me."

We stayed in the classroom talking until it was twilight, then walked to the train station together.

8

It was finally Saturday, the day I'd been looking forward to. I got up early and finished all the chores, then got to work making the lunch for our outing. I'd waffled over the menu but ultimately decided on sandwiches that went well with black tea.

I sprinkled cornstarch over pieces of chicken and panfried them for a low-calorie version of fried chicken. Salad was essential, of course. And some fruit, which is always nice with tea.

Dad had been shut up in his room all morning. When I brought him a cup of tea from the pot I'd made for myself, he was typing on the lone family laptop.

"Working on your novel again?"

"Yeah, the deadline for the *Literary World* New Author Prize is coming up. Oooh, that smells good," he said, turning around in his floor chair to take the cup.

Writing novels is my dad's hobby and form of entertainment, and maybe the whole point of his life. He's been writing them since before I was born, although he's never won a prize. His dream was to support himself as a novelist. That's why he totally neglects the household chores, but it's hard for me to scold him for it.

"I'm going on a date today, so I won't be home for lunch," I told him. "I put some extra sandwiches and stuff in the fridge for you."

"Thanks, I appreciate it. A date, eh? Wait a minute."

He stood up and searched for his wallet. He opened it, frowned, rustled around in the dresser, and took a bill from an envelope.

"Here, your allowance. You keep refusing to take it, but I know there's a limit to what a high school kid can do with the leftover change from the household budget."

"That's okay. I can afford tea and other things I like with the food budget, and I'm grateful that you pay for my commuter pass and phone."

"Of course I do. I'm the one who said you couldn't ride your bike to school. Also, we're on a super-cheap phone plan. Just take the money, okay?"

I stared at the 10,000-yen bill he was holding out.

There's power in money. The power to make people happy. People smile when they eat delicious food, and having things they like brings small joys and vitality to everyday life. All the more reason to use money carefully.

"Okay, I'll use half. And I'll spend the rest on something good for dinner. How about your favorite, sukiyaki? There won't be Chinese cabbage this time of year, but I can get some good meat."

"Come on, you can use more than that. But if that'll make you compromise, I'll take it. We'll have a feast tonight with the other half, then," Dad said, thrusting the money toward me as if saying to take it quickly.

"Thanks. Tonight's gonna be good."

"Have fun today, Tooru."

I took the bill, thanked him again, and went back to my room. I slipped the money into the wallet I'd been using since junior high. Then I quickly wrapped up some chores and pulled out the picnic basket my sister had adored from the closet.

It was a sturdy, caramel-colored rattan basket. I nestled our bentos and a thermos inside. I decided to leave the house at eleven, although that would get me there a little early. There was a large park about fifteen minutes from my house on foot. It was famous for its cherry blossom trees and always packed with people in spring. I'd arranged to meet Hino there in front of the fountain at noon. I thought about taking my bike, but I wanted to enjoy the breeze, so I decided to walk.

I ended up arriving more than half an hour early. There were people around, but it wasn't too crowded. I sat on a bench with a view of the fountain and took out the book I'd tucked into the basket. Ever since I was little, I've liked reading outside on my days off from school. I guess I was a kind of odd kid. Reading outside was enough to get me weirdly excited, so even though I didn't have a big family, I didn't feel too lonely.

Also, I knew that if I got lost in a book and kept reading until dusk to the point that I looked up in surprise and realized how late it was, someone would always come find me.

"I thought you'd be here!"

Someone would come walking toward me, the purple and crimson sky behind them.

My sister.

"Is that you, Tooru?"

I looked up from my book. Hino was standing in front of me, looking slightly nervous. According to the clock in the park, more than half an hour had passed.

"Yep, it's me."

"Whew. Sorry, I'm not used to seeing you in street clothes, so I wasn't sure."

"No worries. I'm the one who should apologize. I didn't realize you'd arrived."

I noticed she was dressed differently than usual. She had on a white shirt and a long, soft-looking green skirt. I realized I'd never seen her in anything but her uniform before. As I was staring at her, she noticed the picnic basket.

"Is that our lunch? Wow, this is the first time I've ever seen such a proper picnic basket before!"

"This? My sister got it for cheap at a bazaar or something ages ago."

"Your sister? I'm sorry. Did you tell me about her before? I thought it was just you and your dad…"

"Yeah, right now it's the two of us, but until recently, my older sister lived with us. It's not that she died or anything…"

Hino must have sensed that I was having trouble explaining, because she said cheerfully, "Ah, got it. Anyway, I'm starving! Where should we eat? Of course, I'm the one who made us wait until noon!"

She smiled brilliantly. Sometimes, when a dazzling light shines on you, it creates equally dark shadows, and you get caught in those shadows. Like when a person who's lost a loved one sees a happy family together. Yet the light shining from Hino didn't make me feel lonely. Maybe some tragedies in the world only exist inside of a person. I smiled back at her and stood up.

We blended in with the Saturday park scene. Luckily for us, a spot was open under a tree on the lawn, so we could sit out of the direct sunlight. I spread out the picnic blanket and set our bentos out as families played in the distance. Before we ate, Hino took a picture of our lunch.

"Ahhh, that was delicious. You're amazing, Tooru. You're such a good cook."

We were talking and having fun, and time flew by. It was a budget lunch, but I was glad she'd liked it.

"It's nothing special. I just used what we had around the house."

"But it was seriously good. You'll make a great husband."

"You'd make a good wife, too…I think."

"What makes you unsure?"

I smiled wryly. Breathing in the fresh air, I looked up at the sky. I felt like a storybook character. I was connected to the person sitting next to me by an unusual bond. We definitely didn't *like* each other. Still, I was grateful to have someone to spend the day off with. Grateful and happy.

We chatted about nothing in particular, smiled, admired each other, and gazed around at the park. Eventually, we fell silent. I didn't know how she felt, but to me, the silence wasn't uncomfortable.

"It's funny," Hino mumbled. I looked at her. She noticed me staring and smiled softly.

"What?"

"Nothing, it's just strange. Like, really strange. I don't feel anxious or uneasy. Even when we're not talking, I don't feel bored or uncomfortable. I even feel like we've been quietly accumulating days like this together."

Something was trembling in a part of her I couldn't see, a part I hadn't even realized was there.

For a second, I was happy.

I was glad that we had built something together, even if it was small. I closed my eyes. The sensation spread a little. I savored it. The warmth of the sun. The smell of the grass. Even the breathing of the person next to me. A strong wind blew, and I opened my eyes. Hino was holding back her long hair. In that moment, I wanted to tell her.

I realized I couldn't lie about my feelings anymore.

"Is it okay if I fall in love with you?"

The wind had already stopped blowing when I asked her that question. I thought about that moment, which had ended before I finished speaking. So I loved her. I saw it now. Saying it made it feel real. How I felt about you…

Hino turned toward me slowly.

"No, it is not," she said.

"Why not?" I asked. She looked down, like she was tangled in doubt.

"I…"

The wind blew again, as if to carry away her long hair.

"I have a disease. It's called anterograde amnesia. When I go to sleep at night, I forget. I forget everything that happened that day."

Maybe her voice mingled with the wind, because it took a long time to reach me.

Walking Side by Side

1

I begin the day called today with the sound of my phone alarm. At first, I feel suspicious of the distant ringing. Why is my phone ringing? I don't like to be woken up by alarm clocks, I prefer to wake up to natural sunlight. So when I went to bed the night before, I made sure I left the curtains open. Though, for some reason, the alarm on my phone is on anyway. Also, it's in a different place than where I left it. It's on the display shelf across from my bed.

I get out of bed and patter across the floor. Hmm, it's a bit warm today. I wonder what time it is. I turn off the alarm and look at the time.

...Why did the alarm go off this early?

I stayed up till around midnight studying, so I only slept around five hours. But my body feels oddly well rested. I sigh at my phone, which seems to have malfunctioned, but then I remember it's Golden Week. Awesome. Vacation.

I have an easy time falling asleep, but once I'm up, I can't go back to sleep. I decide to go downstairs and make myself a latte. I turn on the light in my room.

I've suffered memory loss from an accident. Read the binder on the desk.

Put my heart and soul into each day.

Start with the binder. It's on the desk.

Outside, the world is still dim. In the faint light, I see notes taped all over my room. A shiver runs down my back as a weird feeling grips me.

What is going on?

The unfamiliar notes are written in my own handwriting. Then I realize there was something off about my phone a minute ago. I hurriedly check the screen. The date is wrong.

Yesterday should have been April 26. I remember because it was the first day of Golden Week. But the date on the phone is more than a month later. And there are all those strange notes.

An accident? Memory loss?

Feeling overwhelmed, I begin to panic. I hear footsteps in the hall and turn toward the door as someone knocks. When I answer, Mom opens the door, carrying a tray with a mug on it. She walks in, looking solemn. What? Why?

I have a lot of questions, but first I ask about the notes. She says with difficulty, "Maori. You·had an accident. It made you lose your memory."

As she tells me the details, I'm stunned.

Now I remember. I did get in an accident. It definitely happened yesterday.

But to everyone else, it wasn't yesterday. It was weeks ago.

This can't be true. I feel my face stiffen. Yet, no matter how hard I try to recall what happened the day before, all I can remember is the "yesterday" when the accident happened. I wondered if Mom was lying to me, but she would have no reason to do that.

Which means I really must have suffered memory loss.

To be honest, I can't laugh this one off. I want to, but I can't.

To calm myself down, I sit on the chair and drink the cinnamon latte Mom brought. My favorite. Except it doesn't soothe me like it usually does. I'm shaking. Mom watches me with a pained expression. She tells me I do the same thing every day. I look at the binder and journal I keep.

Apparently, I get up early every day to read it. That's why I have to go to bed by ten at the latest. It seems Mom has adjusted her schedule to match mine. She leaves me to myself, saying she'll be downstairs if I have any questions.

I turn to the binder on my desk. I don't recognize it, but it has a simple design that I like. You can add pages, and there are tabs sticking out so you can find the topic you want right away.

According to Mom, I usually take notes on my phone, but I write down the important stuff in the binder. That way I don't have to worry about ever losing the data.

I reach out nervously for it. The first tab says "Important." This section lists essential information, like the fact that I got in an accident, the nature of my disability, and the fact that only my parents, Izumi, and my teachers know what happened. It seems I haven't told my classmates that I have amnesia. The reason is written in the binder.

It says that when my parents and I consulted with the school about my disability, we were told that there's a national law for the disabled stipulating that so long as I attend school and meet the required amount of days, I'll be able to graduate. It also seems the school administrators brought up the risks of having memory loss. I'd never have thought of this myself, but if rumors about my disability spread, it could be dangerous. No matter what happens, no matter what anyone does to me, I won't remember. The next day, I'll forget everything. If other students were to hear of this, they may visit my classroom to catch a glimpse of me. Not just that; these days, information could easily spread beyond my own school.

Of course, it's not like the world is filled with nothing but bad people. There are lots of good people out there. If I told my classmates, I'm sure they'd be considerate of me. However, there's no guarantee they'd keep quiet. If anything happened, it would be too late to fix. That fear could weigh on me and affect my mental state.

The important thing is to try to avoid stress, enjoy life, and keep calm. Apparently, that's what the doctor said. That's why I avoid hanging out with anyone other than Izumi, it seems.

By the time I'm done reading the "Important" section, I can hardly breathe. The future that was open before me has suddenly disappeared, leaving me alone in the dark. I want to stop reading. The weight of reality feels like it's going to crush me.

But I continue because there was also a glimmer of hope on that page.

Despite the state I'm in, I have a boyfriend. Please read the section labeled "My Boyfriend" and the diary entries starting on May 27. You'll find information about him there.

I reread those lines, deep in thought.

Boyfriend? How, though? Given the circumstances, what could that mean?

I pluck up the courage to read those pages.

His name is Tooru Kamiya, and he's in a different class from me. I barely remember seeing him before. I think he's pale and skinny. According to my notes, there are photos and videos of him in a folder on my phone.

When I look at them, they confirm my hunch as to who he is. Among them are pictures of us close together like a typical couple. The section on him gives a timeline of our relationship.

One day, out of the blue, Kamiya stopped me in the hallway after class. He then asked me to go behind the school with him, where he confessed he liked me. I also had written down that it seemed more like someone had forced him to do it rather than a confession of his genuine feelings. Normally, I would've rejected him. But, supposedly, I had a flash of genius and decided to take advantage of his declaration of feelings. I wanted to see if I could do something new, even with my memory loss.

Up till then, it seems I'd been shocked that I couldn't build up anything over time. The days passed without me accomplishing anything. That was why I jumped in headfirst, apparently.

I gave him three conditions for dating.

First, we don't talk to each other until after school.

Second, when we contact each other, we keep it short.

Third, he's not allowed to fall in love with me.

I'd written down my reasons for each one in the binder.

For the first rule, I thought I'd need time each day to read my notes and get my thoughts in order, especially since I'm still attending school.

Then, for the second one, if he sent me a flood of messages, I wouldn't have time to respond, and I could get in trouble if he brought up something that happened in the past.

Last, even if we were dating, I was sure we'd break up eventually because of my situation, so I didn't want us to develop feelings for each other. This was going to be a fake relationship.

Next, I read over Kamiya's profile.

I'd written down everything from his birthday, family structure, blood type, and favorite author to his personality. Downfallen aristocrat, Mum, importance of being sanitary. I wonder what he means by "sanitary," but there's an explanation that follows. Apparently, you can fake being clean, but you can't fake sanitation. I couldn't help feeling a little impressed, and I became mildly interested in him.

I reach bravely for the journal.

While the binder is for summarizing important points, the journal seems to be a diary. The entries start from the day after the accident and continue to the present. There are weekly summaries so I can read them more quickly.

The mood of the journal is quite different from the binder. It's written freely, without any formalities. I don't have a lot of time, so I glance over the summaries first. It seems I've been trying to stick to the routine I had before so that no one notices I'm different.

I finish reading the summaries of everything that happened before I met my boyfriend. When I finally get to May 27, I start reading the individual entries.

"After school." "Date." "My boyfriend." "Izumi." "Black tea." I lose myself in reading, hardly believing the entries are about my own life. Naturally, it's not all rainbows and butterflies. The summaries included some depressing stuff, like how I worked hard to get into the advanced class and now it's meaningless, or things about friends, or the fact that my memory loss wasn't getting any better.

However, after I started dating Kamiya, the journal is full of positive, happy things. What we talked about, how cute he looked at this moment or that. Knowing that it was comfortable between us to not worry about all the little things helped the current me who wasn't normal to feel braver every day.

By now the sun is up, and it's already seven.

After I finish reading, my fear about my memory loss has receded a little. I go downstairs to the living room, where Dad is reading the newspaper. He looks the same as yesterday, but I can tell he's a little nervous. He puts the paper down and smiles at me.

I wonder if he does that every day.

"Um, I'm sorry about all of this, Dad," I say, lowering my head. He gets up in a flurry.

"You have nothing to apologize for! Right, honey?" he says, glancing at Mom. "If you hadn't saved that child, they might have died. You did a wonderful thing. And memory loss might be rare, but there have been similar cases. It could take time, but there's a chance you'll recover. Let's take this slowly."

When I think about how he and Mom must say all of this to me every day, I feel bad. But looking depressed would only make it worse, so I nod cheerfully. It must have reassured Dad because he gives me a hearty, slightly unnatural smile.

We eat breakfast together, and I go back to my room. I look in my binder and see that today, Saturday, I have a date with my fake boyfriend at the park at noon.

Wow, a date. Very impressive!

As I'm trying to decide what to wear, Izumi calls.

"Hi, Maori. You have a date with Kamiya today, right? Are you gonna be okay?"

I must have told her about my plans yesterday.

"I'm sorry I've dragged you into all of this, Izumi," I say.

"Dragged me into it? If you mean your memory loss, don't worry about it. I only do what I can and what I want to do," she replies. I'm grateful for her nonchalant words.

Izumi isn't the type who's easy to befriend and become close with. But once she's decided to let you into her world, she's super kind.

"Thanks for saying that. I'm trying to figure out what to wear today."

"Don't ask me."

"Huh?"

"Don't rub my nose in your happy love story."

"I'm not!"

Apparently, my past selves haven't told Izumi that my boyfriend and I aren't a real couple. Most likely because I've already caused her enough trouble, and since I'm in this relationship for selfish reasons, I feel like my past selves should be dealing with it on their own.

I try on a bunch of different outfits and finally decide on one.

In the time I have left, I read more of the binder and journal. I seem to have been fairly depressed at first, but I adjusted to "now" with surprising ease.

I tell Mom I'm going out, and Dad's eyes widen when I tell him I have a date. Dad really wants to drive me there, but I turn him down with a smile and go by train and foot instead. As I walk toward the park, I think about various things.

I'm managing fairly well. I've got all the data on my boyfriend logged in my brain. I look up. The weather is beautiful, and the sunbeams almost seem to glow as they pour down.

Maybe I can go on living an ordinary life.

Although, if I don't write down what happens today...I guess it will disappear.

There's a guy at the spot where we agreed to meet who appears to be my boyfriend, based on the photos I looked at. He's hard to recognize in his street clothes, but he has on a crisp white shirt, freshly washed sneakers, and black jeans without a single pill on them. He exudes a "sanitary" aura.

"Is that you, Tooru?"

He looks up from his book.

"Yep, it's me."

"Whew. Sorry, I'm not used to seeing you in street clothes, so I wasn't sure."

He seems to believe my excuse.

Since I keep my memory loss a secret, I haven't told him about it. I wonder if I'll tell him one day. Or maybe we'll break up before that happens. An emotion washes over me, and I notice the picnic basket next to him. Based on our conversation after that, it seems he has an older sister. The basket belongs to her. She didn't die, but he seems sad when he talks about her. I want to cheer him up, so I say I'm hungry, and he smiles.

After that, we act like a couple. Under a tree, we spread a blanket on the top of the carpet of grass and stretch our legs. We eat the lunch my boyfriend made as we watch families play in the distance. I wolf down the colorful, vegetable-packed sandwiches. The low-calorie side dishes are delicious, too.

"You'll make a good husband," I say.

"You'd make a good wife, too… I think."

"What makes you unsure?"

I turn to him, and he smiles. What is this weird feeling? This total stranger accepts me. However, that's not all. I accept him, too, as if it was completely natural. It's a warm feeling. I'm surprised people can be like this together.

Even if I can only remember a single day, and I only know him based on information I've recorded, if he knows me, and he has memories of the time we spent together, he can look at me with those gentle eyes. I feel oddly at ease. I don't even feel uncomfortable when there's silence between us.

"It's funny," I say, my thoughts spilling out.

"What?" he asks. Our eyes meet for a second, and then I look away.

"Nothing, it's just strange. Like, really strange. I don't feel anxious or uneasy. Even when we're not talking, I don't feel bored or uncomfortable. I even feel like we've been quietly accumulating days like this together."

We look out at the gentle sunshine, watching time go by.

I think about the god who made me like this. I'm certain God doesn't care about humans. That God exists in a place beyond human standards, where good and bad don't exist. But maybe God is kind. Just maybe.

The wind blows furiously. I feel my boyfriend watching me as I try to keep my hair in place. By the time I notice, he's already speaking.

"Is it okay if I fall in love with you?"

I turn slowly toward him. He's looking at me with a serious expression. I feel like I'm going to cry.

Ah, I knew it. God is vicious and cruel.

2

Anterograde amnesia. I'd never heard of it before, but Hino explained the symptoms.

Simply put, it means you can't accumulate new memories. Brain trauma from an accident affected the part responsible for storing memories, and it is now dysfunctional. She's able to maintain her memories from when she wakes up in the morning until she goes to sleep at night, but when she falls asleep and her brain begins to process them, the memories from that day are erased. The next morning, nothing is left. Her memories are reset, and she returns to being herself from the day before the accident.

As she talked, images of her flickered across my mind. How she always took notes on her phone and was always snapping pictures. How she looked at me with great interest when we met for our date. All of it was connected to her amnesia. That wasn't all. The established three conditions were as well.

When she finished telling me how she strung together her memories using the information from her binder and journal, she looked on the verge of tears. I stared at her dumbfounded.

"I'm sorry to get you involved in this weird situation," she said. She hadn't meant to tell me.

"Weird situation?"

Her face clouded over.

"Yes."

"What do you mean?"

"I had the upper hand when you said you liked me, but you didn't actually, so I took advantage of it. I wanted to see if I could still do something new."

"I'm the one who should apologize for saying I liked you when I didn't. That's why…"

I wanted to say something to cheer her up, but the words stuck in my throat. Hino still looked glum. I didn't want to see her like that. I wanted her to smile.

"Does anyone else know about your memory loss?" I finally managed to say. Everything I'd said so far was either a question or a denial. Hino was looking down.

"Yes. Izumi, my parents, and my teachers."

That was a small list. She said it was because of the unexpected dangers of memory loss. I was shocked to hear her say that, but it was true. Having people knowing about her amnesia would be risky.

When she finished speaking, she cast her eyes down again. I didn't want to make her feel bad. I didn't want to keep asking all these questions. Was there anything I could do as her boyfriend, even if I was a fake one? I had to think of something.

I knew the answer. It came to me so easily that it didn't even seem like my own idea.

Do you know a proverb that goes "you can't hide a cough" and something?

I thought back to Shimokawa's words. What had caused it? Was it her smile that seemed special in my world of scarce smiles? Or because she was beautiful? Or when I realized she was hiding something? My love for her had materialized quite unexpectedly. By the time I realized, she was the only thing I could see.

"If you don't write down what happened today in your binder or your journal, tomorrow you won't know about this, right?"

"Right. I'll wake up like I did today, thinking the accident happened yesterday. If I don't write it down… Wait a second, Tooru."

She finally looked up.

I'd experienced many emotions in my life, both positive and negative. Joy, anguish, sorrow, peace. Still, I couldn't remember ever experiencing a feeling as pure as what I felt in that moment.

I surprised myself again.

Because I'm with you. Because I want to be with you.

"Then don't write down that you told me about your memory loss. And don't write that I confessed and said I love you."

I said it very quietly, omitting the question mark.

Hino looked surprised. I tried to force a smile.

"I broke the rules, after all. If…*if* you're still okay with me being your fake boyfriend, then you'd probably prefer not to know I have real feelings for you, right? And if you didn't intend to tell me about your illness but the fact that you did makes you even slightly worried, then you should forget you told me. From now on, I'll pretend I don't notice. What do you think?"

She didn't answer right away. I could see the uncertainty in her face.

"I feel like I'm getting the long end of the stick," she said.

"That's not true. I…"

For a few seconds, I thought about what had changed me. To me, love was a mysterious feeling. I'd heard kids talking about it in class, but it seemed like something that existed in a different world. Now, so naturally, like it was nothing at all, I had fallen in love with Hino. I loved her smile, the way she said silly things, the way she was herself but at the same time thoughtful about other people. I could never express all the reasons I loved her. I even felt puzzled by my own first love. Except, what was the point in telling her all of that? What if it became a burden to her?

"I had a boring life before I met you," I said. "As long as I can keep spending time with you, I don't care if I'm your fake boyfriend. It seems like we should just pretend none of this happened today."

I could hear families making an amiable racket in the distance. She and I sat some ways away from them. I gazed up at the clouds. I could keenly feel how artificial I was when I watched those clouds floating past, so utterly free and natural.

"Is that really okay with you, Tooru?"

When I looked down again, Hino was watching me with a worried expression.

"Yeah. I like hanging out with you. Of course, it all depends on what you think."

She sank into deep thought.

Maybe in the future, this decision would cause us suffering. But still, I prayed my wish would be granted and my feelings would reach her.

She hesitated for a long time. She pursed her lips, then finally said, "All right. I won't write down what happened today. I'll forget it."

Forget it. What she meant by those words was very different from what most people meant by them. She truly won't remember. If she didn't leave a record of her actions, if she didn't write down her path through the world, they would vanish.

"Thank you," I said.

"No, I'm sorry…to make you take on so much."

"It's no big deal. I'm delighted to have a beautiful girl as my fake girlfriend."

I was trying to be silly and laugh it off, but my words fell flat.

I offered her some tea, and we both drank some from paper cups. I asked her to tell me more about her memory loss, and she readily agreed. Normally, her memories are reset when she sleeps, but apparently, if she stays up all night, they last to the next day. Though she said that was kind of pointless. She had tried it with Wataya and learned firsthand that humans can't live without sleep.

All of her teachers, including her homeroom teacher, knew about her condition and never called on her in class. She turned in all her homework blank. She sat for her tests, but it didn't matter if she got all the answers wrong. She said discovering day after day that she'd lost her memory was hard, but as long as she attended class, she would be able to graduate. She hadn't yet considered what she would do after that.

We'd met at noon and decided to leave at three, though it was a little earlier than planned. On the way back, I said to her, "I hope you really won't write anything down in your binder or journal. I'll know if you do. You're easy to read."

"I won't."

Her face looked paler and more fragile than I had ever seen it before. The current Hino was merely one page among the infinite pages that make up a life.

"Tooru…thank you for today. You really are a kind person."

Me, kind? I wasn't so sure.

"No, thank you. Also…"

I was going to ask if it would bother her if I kept loving her, but I decided not to. She was waiting for me to finish my sentence. I shook my head.

"Nothing. I'll walk you to the train station."

After I dropped her off, I figured I would go home, carrying the now-light picnic basket. Except Dad was in the apartment, and I'd told him I was going on a date. If I came home early, and feeling down to boot, he might worry about me.

I decided to walk to another park, where I sat on a bench and read my book. However, the words wouldn't stick. I reread the same line again and again. I'm not sure how long I sat there like that, going in circles.

At five o'clock, the evening music played. I stopped by a butcher in the shopping arcade that I hardly ever went to, bought some beef, and went home. Dad seemed happy about the sukiyaki I made and reported he'd made progress on his writing.

"And how was your day?" he asked. For a second, I grew serious.

"She loved the bento I made," I managed to say. He smiled happily.

"Glad to hear it. Hey, have some more of this meat. When I win that new author prize, let's celebrate together, the three of us. What do you say, Tooru?"

Despite his low alcohol tolerance, Dad drank again and fell asleep early. As I washed the dishes, I thought about a lot of things.

What in the world did it mean to love someone? Why do people fall in love? Why, when falling in love can be painful and sad sometimes?

There were no answers to my questions. There was only the endless monotonous clatter of the dishes being washed.

3

Sunday was my last day with Shimokawa.

His new school was overseas. I wanted to see him off at the airport, but he had felt bad about me spending the train fare to get there, so he suggested we meet at a nearby station where he could catch the express train instead. I thought I was getting there fairly early, but he was already waiting in front of the ticket gates.

"Sorry to keep you waiting. You got here early?" I said.

He didn't say anything. I wondered why, but then he started talking about the bully. Choosing his words carefully, he said he'd told the teachers the guy was squeezing money from him.

"Well…a few minutes ago, he came to return the money. The day after I told the teachers, he talked to me after school. I told him I'd taken the cash from my New Year's money and I didn't need it, but he said he'd return it. I got here early today because I'd agreed to meet him. He'd scraped it together from a part-time job, and he borrowed from his brother, too."

I couldn't help glancing around, even though I knew he wasn't there anymore. I should respond, but my mind still felt somewhat sluggish after what had happened with Hino the day before. Then I remembered that I'd seen the guy alone in class, reading a magazine with job listings.

"Huh. So…you did the right thing and went to the teachers."

I didn't mention that I'd heard the story from the bully already.

"Yeah. There's probably lots of reasons I was still getting picked on in high school. Probably because I'm dumb and fat…but I was too embarrassed to tell anyone. That ended up causing you a lot of trouble. I knew it was time for me to be brave. But I didn't realize I'd mess up his life. He said his friends abandoned him, and now he's all alone in class."

I was stunned by the way Shimokawa resisted saying the guy had gotten what he'd deserved and instead was genuinely worried about how it affected him. I hadn't known Shimokawa for long, but he felt like a really important, irreplaceable friend to me.

We tried to talk like normal, but it didn't go very well. Ultimately, he broke the silence.

"Kamiya, thanks for being friends with me," he said. I looked up. "You'll say it's not true, but I think you're a great person. You pretend you don't have anything, but you have the things that matter. Like kindness."

I couldn't help becoming serious. I'd never heard him talk like this before.

"My dad says it's much harder to become a kind person than an important one. That means you're much more admirable than some VIP. Maybe it's rude of me to say this, but even though you've got a tough life, you're not warped. Another thing my dad said is that people who've had it hard usually become servile or mean. But you're not. You're really and truly kind."

His words overlapped with what Hino had said the day before we parted.

You really are a kind person.

Kind? No, not me. Only in a half-assed, not-at-all-praiseworthy way. I was going to say that, but I didn't.

"Don't suffer, okay, Shimokawa? Go become an important, admirable person," I said jokingly, although I really meant it. He smiled.

"I'll try," he said. "I'm sorry, Kamiya. I'm gonna start crying soon, so I better go. Thank you. I haven't known you long, but I won't forget you. Thanks for sticking by me."

He held out his beautiful hand. I looked down at my own worriedly. I felt bad making him shake a hand like mine, but I held it out anyway. He gripped it firmly. I gripped his back.

"Wherever you wind up, live strong, Shimokawa."

"I'll give it my best."

"Just kidding. You don't have to stay strong."

"Careful; you'll ruin my resolve."

"And why not try to lose a few pounds? You're a handsome guy, you know."

"Really, you think so? I'll give it a go, then."

He smiled shyly, and I let go of his hand.

"Well, my family is waiting at the airport," he said. "Hope things go well with Hino."

His words shook me a little, but I nodded in reply. He smiled jovially. Then he turned and left, walking toward his new life beyond the ticket gate. He looked back and gave a big wave. I waved back.

"Till we meet again!" Shimokawa shouted. "I'll be a changed man! I'll get in shape and date a great girl like Hino, and we can talk about our relationships."

All I could manage was a weak "Yeah."

When I got home, I could hear Dad typing. He must have been working on his novel. This was my life. I looked up at the low ceiling.

I did some cleaning around the house, and it soon became noon. I didn't feel like eating, but I made something simple, and the two of us ate it quietly. By the afternoon, I felt drained and lay down in bed. I checked my phone and saw I had a message. I thought it would be from Shimokawa, but it was from Wataya. I didn't read it or respond. It was that kind of day.

4

It was break time after second period on Monday. I was thinking about how big the classroom felt without Shimokawa when I noticed someone watching me. It was Wataya, looking in from the hall with a disgruntled expression, her arms crossed. When she saw me looking back at her, she gestured for me to come outside. I walked out of the classroom, my mind blank. I followed her to the corner of the hallway where we'd first talked.

"Why'd you ignore my message?" she asked after stopping and glancing behind her.

"I'm sorry; I didn't know you texted me. I don't check my phone very often."

"So you haven't read it yet?"

"I think my phone is in my bag. I'll check it later."

I hadn't read it, but I did know she'd sent it. I wondered why I'd lied to her. She swept the hair back from her temples, revealing her well-shaped ears.

"That's fine. There's no point. I was just wondering…if something happened with Maori."

"With Hino?" I answered nonchalantly. "Not particularly. On Saturday, we went to the park. We did end the date a little early. Why? Did something happen?"

She sized me up.

"Maori and I talk on the phone on days we don't see each other. We talked on Saturday night, and she wasn't herself."

"How so?"

"She was talking a lot."

"Doesn't she always?"

"This was different. When something tough or sad happens, she always talks more. I've known that for ages, and I don't think I misread her."

I could tell how much she cared about Hino from her concerned tone. Based on what she'd said, it seemed Hino hadn't told her I'd said I loved her or that she'd told me about her memory loss or that I'd asked her not to write it in her notebook. But had she really not written it down?

"Even if you're right, what are the chances it's related to me?"

Why was I being such a jerk? I wasn't my usual self today. Wataya raised her eyebrows suspiciously.

"How should I put this? Maori's family cares a lot about her. It's not to an excessive degree, though, and they're sensible. So I don't think this has to do with her family. Which leaves just you."

Hino's situation hit me all over again. The way Wataya was talking so carefully made Hino's illness and her efforts to hide that much more real to me. And just like Wataya was hiding Hino's condition from me, I hid the truth from her, pretending nothing had changed.

"I don't think anything odd happened on Saturday," I said. "But you never know what people are thinking. I'll bring it up casually when I see her after school today. If you want, you can hang out with us."

"I... No, that's fine. I'm sorry. I'm being weird again. Will you tell me if anything seems wrong when you see her? She seemed okay so far today, but you're her boyfriend, so she might be different around you."

"I'll let you know."

By then, break was over. During the other breaks, I didn't have anything to do, so I finished some homework and studied so I'd have more free time at home. I felt like I'd come up with a good strategy for how to spend my time between classes now that Shimokawa was gone. When I glanced over at the bully, he was alone like me, working on something.

After school, I waited for Hino in the empty classroom.

"Aha, found you! Hi, boyfriend!"

She'd said she hardly even noticed me before her accident. Most likely, she'd identified me just now based on a photo. She probably wouldn't notice if someone who looked like me was here instead, pretending to be me. Those were the absurd scenarios going through my mind as I greeted her.

"Hi, honey," I said.

"Hey, I thought you didn't like that mushy stuff," she answered. So she even wrote down little details like that. I hadn't said it to test her but instead in an attempt to cheer myself up.

"I thought I'd give it a try," I said.

"That must be why you look so tense," she answered bemusedly, surveying my face. I'd always found that habit of hers strange, but now it made sense. I passionately returned her gaze. She gave me a surprised look.

"Saturday," I said, smiling and trying to sound natural.

"What?"

"Thanks for Saturday. I had fun."

She paused very briefly, then said exaggeratedly, "Oh, right, right. Me too! The bento was so good. As your girlfriend, I'd like to cook for you next time, but sorry, I'm awful at that kind of thing."

"I suspected as much."

"Hey, that's rude!"

"You said so yourself!"

"It's different when I say it than when you do."

I looked at her smile, as pure as fresh water, and decided that she seemed to have followed through on her promise.

She hadn't written down that I told her I loved her or that she told me about her memory loss. I could probably rest assured about that.

I would keep my feelings to myself and pretend I didn't notice her amnesia. I would let the little oddities slide. I was fairly sure that was what she wanted.

"So, boyfriend, what should we do today?"

Maybe the reason she always called me "boyfriend" at first when we met was that she wasn't used to saying my name.

"What do you want to do, girlfriend?"

"Me?"

"Yes, you."

"Hmm… Oh yes! I'd like to ride a bike together. Isn't that what all couples dream of?"

I'd been slightly worried about whether I'd manage to be my usual self when we met. But it was easy. Her innocent way of talking made me smile without realizing it. I had to switch gears. I couldn't dwell on what had happened over the weekend. This was the path I had chosen. To keep loving her. To stay by her side. To not tell her how I felt.

"Riding two to a bike is illegal, so that's out. Think of something more proper."

"How about an after-school date?"

"That's not a bad idea. Should we stop somewhere on the way to the station?"

"A family restaurant!"

I couldn't help but laugh at her instant response. The block of ice in my heart started to melt. Every moment I spent with her made me so happy. The sensation was undeniable. Being a fake couple didn't change anything. It didn't change my level of happiness. It didn't change my love for her. Nothing. I didn't need any reward other than this feeling.

"I'll take care of the bill."

"Shoot, you beat me to it! It's going to be expensive; do you mind? Of course, I'll pay for my half, and I'd be happy to pay yours, too, to thank you for dating me."

"It's no problem. I got some extra cash recently. Anything else you want to do?"

"Flirt at the video arcade."

"I'm not going to flirt, but I'll get you a toy from a claw machine."

"Go to the aquarium."

"That's got to be on the weekend, but okay."

"How about going to an amusement park?"

"Good idea."

"Oh, also, karaoke!"

"Only if we invite Wataya."

"You don't want to go as a couple?"

"I mean, it'll be just us in that room. I'd get shy."

"So the downfallen aristocrat is shy?"

"Anyway, what else?"

"Maybe a library date or studying together for a test?"

I couldn't hide my surprise at how long her list was. When she went to sleep, she forgot everything that had happened that day. She couldn't build up her experiences day by day. How hopeless would that feel? How painful? Time had left her behind, all alone, and stolen her future. If that was how it was going to be, then I wanted to fill her journal with happy memories so that tomorrow's Hino could look forward to everyday life, even a little.

I wanted the Hinos of the next day and the next to read those journal entries and feel a little braver. I wanted her fear of the future to lessen, even a little.

"That's a good list. Let's do all those things one by one. We'll start with…I know! We'll start with a bang by riding two to a bike!" I said enthusiastically. She looked surprised.

"Really? Is it okay? You take the train to school like me. Where are we gonna get a bike?"

Let's start living in a new way, a more fun way. If anything can be called hope, that can. Right, Hino?

With those thoughts on my mind, an unaccustomed grin spread across my face. I wanted to tell her without words that falling in love was making my life better.

5

Hino and I sneaked toward the abandoned school bike-parking area.

Since we both take the train to school, neither of us had a bike parked there. Except I'd heard someone in my class say that the parking space wasn't very well managed, and there were always a couple of unlocked bikes lying around. No one knew if they'd been left behind by students who graduated or if someone had stolen them and ditched them there.

Hino and I scanned the lot for those rumored abandoned bikes. It took a while, but eventually we found one.

"Aww, look, it's got a flat," she said dejectedly.

At that moment, I wanted to do whatever I could for her and to fill her journal with fun memories.

"Have no fear, Hino," I declared. "I'll show you the kind of man your boyfriend is. If there's a hole, I'll fix it, and if there isn't, I'll borrow a pump and inflate it. Nothing to it. Right?"

"What's with the transformation? You seem very capable all of a sudden."

"Leave it to me," I said, smiling boldly.

The two of us went to the custodian's office and borrowed a pump. Unfortunately, the air didn't stay inside for very long, and the tire deflated again. Normally, the custodian would fix a flat for students, but I had no idea who this bike belonged to, and it was missing the school commuter sticker. So it was a slim chance he would fix this one. I decided to try my hand at it.

I asked Hino if she had scissors and double-sided tape.

"I'm pretty sure there's some in the teacher's desk in my classroom," she answered. There was a bucket I needed from my own classroom, too. We decided to split up to get the equipment.

"What are you going to do?" Hino asked, her bubbly voice as bouncy as her steps as she walked down the hall after we'd changed to our indoor shoes.

"Something interesting," I said with a smirk.

In my classroom, I opened the cleaning-supply locker, helped myself to the bucket, and went back out. Hino was waiting farther down the hallway. I smiled the crafty smile of a man with a plan, and she did the same. She seemed to have found what she was looking for.

I stopped to fill the pail with water, then hurried back to the bike-parking area with Hino. I took off the tire and submerged the tube in the water. The trail of bubbles led me to the hole. Meanwhile, Hino was following my instructions to cut a Band-Aid-sized piece out of one of my plastic folders and cover one side of it with double-sided tape.

The rest was easy. I pressed the piece of plastic onto the hole, reinforced it with the tape, and put the tire back on and inflated it. This time, the pressure held.

"You're so handy! My boyfriend is amazing!" she shouted excitedly.

I punched my palm proudly. She glanced eagerly at the bike. I'm not poor for nothing. I've got all sorts of tricks like this up my sleeve.

"So, Hino, are you ready?" I asked.

Fixing the flat wasn't the main event, after all. She smiled giddily.

"You mean what I was talking about?"

I smiled at her.

"Yup, that."

She grinned back at me.

"Yes! Go, go, go!"

We were flying down a road between rice fields, both of us on the one bike. I was straddling the seat, pedaling furiously. She was perched on the cargo rack behind me, riding sidesaddle. One of her arms was wrapped around my waist.

We were breaking traffic laws. Technically, traffic regulations. If a police officer or a teacher caught us, we'd definitely get a citation or a stern warning. To top it off, we were possibly riding a stolen bike. So we chose a route far away from the one most students used to get to school.

"Oh my gosh, you're so fast!" Hino screamed.

I pedaled as hard as I could, silently cursing my weak legs. The newly fixed tire showed no sign of deflating. There I was, racing down a road with a girl sitting behind me on a possibly stolen bike.

I was shocked I'd managed to do it. Was this even me?

Now that I thought about it, up till now, I'd always been overly rational and never done anything stupid. In other words, I'd lived a boring life. That kind of life would never fill Hino's journal with fun memories. From now on, I was ready to do anything she wanted, no matter how reckless or crazy, such as riding a bike that might belong to someone else and yelling at the top of my lungs. Insane things. Things she would think were exciting.

"Don't you want to take a video?" I asked loudly to hide that I was short of breath so the wind wouldn't drown out my voice.

"What? Oh, a video? Good idea!"

When we watched it later, it was too shaky to see what was happening. But I could still hear Hino's happy screams. Now and then, I glimpsed my own smiling face glancing over my shoulder.

After we'd ridden up and down the road to her heart's content, we returned the bike. She offered to give me a ride back to school, but I didn't think she would be strong enough. Also, a teacher might catch us, so we pushed it back. Afterward, we walked to the station. She was giddy the whole time.

"What should we do tomorrow?" I asked as the evening sun tinted the streets. She raised her eyebrows.

"What do you mean?"

"After school tomorrow."

"Hmm…," she said pensively. I couldn't help smiling.

"I'm going to show tomorrow's Hino a good time," I said.

I'd gotten a bit too bold and raised her suspicion.

"What?" she asked in surprise, looking me in the eye like she was trying to read my mind.

"What's wrong?" I asked. She hurriedly averted her gaze.

"Nothing. Never mind."

"Anyway, make up your mind by tomorrow after school. Or we could just decide when we meet."

"You seem different, Tooru."

I suppose what she meant was my personality today seemed different from the description she'd written in her journal. I was happy about that difference. She probably didn't have the slightest idea that I knew about her illness.

"I wonder why. Lately, I've really been enjoying hanging out with you. Maybe that makes me seem different."

"Maybe. People are funny, aren't they?"

Then she took out her phone to check something. I stole a glance and saw that she had written a list of all the things she'd said she wanted to do.

"If you want, we can ride a bike together again tomorrow," I said, looking away.

"But wouldn't it be boring for you to do the same thing two days in a row?"

"You'd be doing it two days in a row, too."

"True. You have a point."

A strange feeling of satisfaction came over me.

"I won't be bored. Don't worry about me. As long as I'm with you, I'm happy. Let's do what you want tomorrow. Okay?"

"Okay!"

We ended up riding a bike together again the next day after school. Each day's Hino existed only for that single day.

She smiled just as brightly as the day before, because once again, she felt like she was riding a bike together for the first time. It was easier this time because I didn't have to fix the tire, and since I was with her, I wasn't bored.

I was a little surprised when she wanted to do it a third day in a row, but I guess that day's Hino couldn't resist after reading the journal entry from the day before. If that was the case, then I was glad.

The only difference was that Wataya was with us. She seemed slightly exasperated by our yelps as we rode but also like she found it heartwarming.

"Hey, you hooligans over there! Riding two to a bike is a violation of traffic safety regulations!" she said with a smile. "Please dismount immediately. I repeat, riding two to a bike is against the law. Get off the bike this instant!"

"I've got a deal for you!" Hino shouted back.

"Tell me your conditions!"

"If I give you a ride, will you overlook our violation?"

"What is this, a bribe? I'm shocked! But the offer isn't bad."

Hino took over the driver's seat, and Wataya sat on the cargo rack. Hino started pedaling but couldn't gather speed.

"You need more horsepower, Maori!" Wataya complained.

"Should we try dangling a carrot in front of her?" I joked as she returned, panting.

"Hey! How dare you talk like that to your girlfriend!" she shot back playfully between pants.

At Wataya's insistence, I took the pedals after that. She shouted happily as we flew down the road. Hino seemed to have bounced back enough to complain theatrically.

"You two-timing cheaters! Step away from the bicycle immediately!"

"Sorry, Maori!" Wataya called back. "I'm keeping this downfallen aristocrat. No one can stop a pair of fleeing lovers. Bye!"

"Tooru, I curse you and your children and your children's children!"

I couldn't help laughing. I looked up. The sky was burning crimson like a picture from a storybook.

6

We spent the afternoons that week messing around with the bike, and on Saturday, the three of us went to the aquarium.

We'd agreed to meet at one at the clock tower outside the terminal station downtown. We had to pass through that station to get there, and then the aquarium was another fifteen minutes away by subway.

I'd heard there was a big plaza in the aquarium where we could eat lunch. It would be kind of a late meal, but I packed enough food for all three of us and got to the terminal about half an hour early. I arrived with enough time, as there was a bookstore that I wanted to visit on the thirteenth floor of the shopping mall attached to the station.

Feeling a bit like an oddball with my picnic basket, I got on a crowded elevator to the thirteenth floor and headed for the bookstore. The corridor was surprisingly packed with people milling around and chatting. All of them were holding books. Figuring they must be there for some event, I went to look at a poster on the wall. I was totally unprepared for what I found. I stood rooted to the spot in a daze.

Book launch and signing with Keiko Nishikawa, Akutagawa Prize–nominated author, it read.

A shiver ran down my spine.

I hesitated for an instant, then made a beeline for the bookstore. Staff were herding people into lines. It seemed the signing was taking place inside and people were queuing for it. The event wasn't mentioned in the latest issue of *Literary World*, but it must have been announced online.

It looked like I could skirt the line and walk through the shop to where Nishikawa was signing books. I made my way toward her, my heart pounding. Other people must have had the same idea because a crowd had formed here as well. I pushed my way through, receiving some nasty glares as I barged ahead with my bulky picnic basket, but I didn't have time to apologize.

I was making steady progress. I could see the yellow tape that must be cordoning off the autograph table. Just a little farther. Now I was right in front of it, and there she was.

The author Keiko Nishikawa—my sister.

My throat felt dry. She was sitting on a folding chair at a long table, signing a book that a person in line held out to her. A woman in a dark suit stood next to her. My sister was looking at the person who had bought her book with a smile I'd never seen before.

"Thank you so much," she said, handing it back and shaking their hand. They bowed and stepped away, looking satisfied. I watched silently.

Suddenly, my sister glanced at me.

"…Tooru?"

I wonder what expression I should have made at that moment. I tried to smile, failed, and probably looked idiotic. The next person in line walked up to the table to ask my sister, or rather, Keiko Nishikawa, for her autograph. But she kept looking at me. The woman standing next to her looked confused.

"What's wrong?" she asked.

"Oh…nothing."

My sister hesitated, then smiled at the next person in line. "I'm sorry," she said and whispered something to the woman in the suit. She then shot me a surprised look and nodded.

Keiko Nishikawa went back to signing books. The lady, who looked somewhat older than my sister, walked over to me.

"Hello. I hear you're Nishikawa's little brother."

"Um, yes. I am."

"This event will last awhile, but I think it will be done in about an hour and a half. Can you get a coffee or something and wait? Your sister said she wants to talk to you."

She gave me the name of a café in the mall.

"All right." I nodded.

The woman smiled and glanced at my sister. She walked over to the table, picked up a book from the pile, and gave it to me. Then she smiled again and returned to her post. The people nearby who had overheard our conversation looked curiously at me. I walked away.

In an hour and a half.

I'd agreed to meet her, but I was supposed to hang out with Hino and Wataya. I left the busy store, unsure what to do. I took the elevator to the ground floor. Outside, I filled my lungs with fresh air and walked over to the clock tower. I was still ten minutes early, but Wataya was already there among the crowd of people.

"You're early, Kamiya," she said. "Did you hear? Keiko Nishikawa is doing a signing at the bookstore. I thought I'd stop by, but the line was crazy."

"Actually...Keiko Nishikawa is my sister," I said.

"Is she? Anyway, there were so many people... What? What did you just say?"

I could hardly tell her I'd been joking, so I smiled vaguely. We stared at each other silently as the crowd buzzed around us.

"I'm sorry. I didn't know she was signing books, but when I went up there, I was lucky enough to talk to her. We haven't seen each other in a while. After the signing, we're supposed to meet again."

I hesitated. Wataya seemed to guess what I was getting at.

"I see. Well, these things happen. You go see her; don't worry about us."

I was grateful for her thoughtfulness. I looked at the ground for a minute, then back at her.

"I wanted to tell Hino, too, but my mind's a mess right now, and I feel too guilty to face her. Could I ask you to tell her for me? Oh, and here's the bento. Eat it if you'd like. There might be too much food since I cooked for three, so don't feel like you have to finish it all. After I meet with my sister, I promise I'll come find you guys."

I handed my sister's picnic basket to Wataya.

"You can put it on the ground if it's too heavy," I said, but she said it was fine.

"Don't worry. I'll cover for you with Maori. And thanks for the bento! Do you mind if I tell her your sister is Keiko Nishikawa?"

"Of course not. She's not the type to gossip, and anyway, she's my girlfriend."

"Your girlfriend...yeah."

She looked at me like she wanted to say something else, then smiled.

"At first, I thought you two were dating as a joke or something, but lately, you're really stepping up. I can tell you're trying to make her happy. Although, to me, you seem to be trying a little too hard."

I think she was testing me. She wanted to know if I knew. At least, that was the sense I got.

"Don't tell Hino this," I said.

"Tell her what?"

"I'm in love with her. Maybe that seems obvious, but I truly do love her. If there's something I can do to help her, I want to do it. That sounds arrogant. But if I can make her happy, I want to," I told her quite earnestly. She was quiet for a moment.

"Why can't I tell Maori?" she finally asked.

"Obviously, because I'm embarrassed about it."

"You don't seem like the type to be embarrassed, Kamiya."

The pulsing din of the station crowd seemed to go silent.

"You know about Maori, don't you?" she asked me.

I caught her wavering gaze. I should have seen this coming.

"Yes. I know."

She looked me straight in the eye, perhaps trying to read my true intentions.

"How do you know? She didn't tell you, did she?"

"Yes, she told me. But I asked her not to write it down in her binder or her journal. Today's Hino…doesn't know that I know about her memory loss."

For once, Wataya looked shaken. But she still didn't know we were a fake couple. There was no way she could know about the three conditions.

"You better not tell her I know," I said, trying to cover up my seriousness with a laugh. With that, I turned toward the elevator hall. I could feel her watching me for a long time as I disappeared into the crowd.

7

June 9 (Monday)

Morning at home: as usual.

Homeroom: Announcement about finals. Teacher jokes around (nothing worth noting).

First period break: Izumi asked about my date on Saturday. Told her what was in the journal, although I didn't write down anything special. She acted suspicious.

Second period break: Izumi went somewhere. Probably to my boyfriend's class. Suzuki asked what I was doing after school. I was vague, said I had to do something. She seemed a little annoyed.

Had fun chatting about gaming livestreams, which she likes (make note in "People" section of binder). Saved the situation?

Third period break: Asked Izumi what happened during second period break. She said she thought my boyfriend was lying to her. So, she did go talk to him. Decided maybe she was wrong, since there wasn't anything in my journal.

Fourth period break: Talked with Izumi. She said, "Wow, June sure crept up on me." I tried to joke about how everything creeps up on me. She said I'd made the same joke before, thought that was funny. Better make sure not to say it again (make note in "People" section of binder).

Lunch: Ate lunch with Izumi. She had a homemade BLT. Drool.

Fifth period break: Izumi is obsessed with black tea lately. Said it's because the tea we had at the downfallen aristocrat's (my boyfriend's) was so good. I want some, too.

After school: Went to my boyfriend's class. He called me "honey" shyly. I said I thought he didn't like mushy stuff. He said he was giving it a try. Pretty cute.

He thanked me for Saturday. I apologized for being a bad cook. He said he expected as much. Rude.

Talked about what to do today. He said, "Let's do what my girlfriend wants to do." I suggested various things: riding a bike together, going to a family restaurant, having an after-school date at a game center, karaoke, aquarium on day off, amusement park. He said okay to everything other than riding a bike together (but karaoke only if Izumi comes; he's embarrassed to be alone with me in the room). He said he has some extra spending money.

Then, even though he said he didn't want to earlier because it's illegal, he suggested we ride a bike together. I need to revise my information on him. This guy is up for anything.

We found an abandoned bike, but it had a flat tire. I was disappointed, but the boyfriend said, "Have no fear, Hino. I'll show you the kind of man your boyfriend is." I was a little surprised. No, make that quite a bit.

He got to work fixing it. I helped. I found some scissors and double-sided tape and cut a piece of a plastic file folder. What the heck, right? But he used it to fix the hole. Impressive.

We went to a country road far away from school where no teachers or police would see us and rode the bike together. He pedaled really hard. It was fun. The wind was really strong. I feel happy just remembering it. Ah, youth! It's like the hopelessness I felt this morning never even existed. I'm amazing. I'm impressive. I'm so glad I'm dating him.

Even if I have memory loss, maybe I can enjoy each day like I did today. Riding together was a little scary, and this weird laugh came up from the pit of my stomach. The boyfriend laughed, too. I took a video (see the "My Boyfriend" folder in phone).

After we rode as much as we wanted, we walked it back to

school. He asked what I wanted to do tomorrow. He said, "I'm going to show tomorrow's Hino a good time." That was a surprise. Did he guess I have amnesia? No, he couldn't have, right? He didn't act like he thinks I'm weird. I said he's changed, and he said he just likes to hang out with me. That was nice. I'm a sucker for that look of his.

It's strange that I feel this way even though yesterday he was a stranger. As far as I can tell from this journal, I experience that strangeness every day.

He said we could ride the bike again tomorrow if I want. He doesn't mind doing the same thing two days in a row. The one good thing about the current me is that new stuff is always new.

No matter how many times I've done it, I enjoy it just like it's the first time.

I feel a little more optimistic than before. Boyfriend, thanks for today.

On Saturday morning, I read my recent journal entries after breakfast, blushing a bit at the girlish words. I would never have expected myself to act so giddy.

According to the journal entry after that day, we played around on the bike again. The next day, we invited Izumi, and she rode around on the bike with my boyfriend. I feel embarrassed to be acting so childishly day after day, but I smile in spite of myself.

I review the page labeled "My Boyfriend" in the binder, then pull up the media folders on my phone. Sure enough, there it is: a new folder labeled "My Boyfriend." It's full of photos and videos of Tooru Kamiya.

I choose one and press play. It's dated Monday. I hear my own flirty voice as the video shakes. The twilight scenery passing by. This must be the video I took while we were riding together. I mentioned it in the journal. My boyfriend glances back at me as he pedals. I say something. Anyone could see how much fun we're having. It's a simple, silly video.

I watch it again. The clumsy memory makes me smile.

In the middle of watching, I notice something. Calmly, I accept it. An emotion that's hard to describe as lonely or yearning is sloshing around in the pit of my stomach. Today's me isn't the person in the video. I feel slightly sad as I watch them laugh and yell. I feel something like longing for yesterday's me.

But…maybe I will experience just as much joy and fun today. Thanks to Tooru Kamiya, this guy whose name I hardly even recognize. I smile slightly.

I cheer up and start getting ready. Today, I'm going to the aquarium with my boyfriend and Izumi. Dad's worried about me, so I let him drive me to the station, and from there, I take the train downtown. I arrive five minutes early. I spot Izumi under the clock tower, where we agreed to meet. She's holding a picnic basket.

"Wherever are you going, Izumi? To your grandmother's house in the woods?" I joke. Normally, she would have an instant comeback, but instead, she looks awkward.

"Um…yeah. Actually, I am. I've got a combat knife hidden in here, so if the wolf is wearing a disguise, I can cut the clothes right off that scoundrel."

"You mean the hide, don't you?"

"I'm planning to get myself a nice fur coat for winter."

All the kids in our class say they can't keep up when we joke around like this. But this time, I wonder if she's not feeling well. Her mind seems to be somewhere else. I realize the basket looks similar to the one I saw my boyfriend holding in a picture.

"Hey, isn't that my boyfriend's?" I ask.

"Oh, this? Yeah."

She's obviously upset.

"Well…Kamiya was here just a minute ago," she explains. "He has some family stuff going on, it sounds like."

She tells me the whole story. Keiko Nishikawa is an author he likes.

"She's his sister? I don't know much about literature. Is she famous?"

"She's the top contender for this year's Akutagawa Prize."

"For real?"

This time, when she answers, she sounds like her usual self.

"I think so. After the nomination was announced, they rushed out the paperback version, which caused a pretty incredible amount of buzz. I think all literature is about the chasm between oneself and the world…"

She goes on to give a passionate review of the book. Izumi is as tough on other people as she is on herself. If she's praising this book, it must be good. And my boyfriend's sister wrote it.

"I'm so curious about her. Are there any photos of her?"

"She never makes public appearances. They didn't even include a picture in the magazine when she won the New Author Prize, so I guess she really hates photos. I was curious, so I went up to get a glimpse.

Sorry to say this, but she's nothing like Kamiya. She's a cool beauty. The signing event was insanely packed, though. Everyone's going to freak out if she wins the Akutagawa Prize."

"Interesting. So my boyfriend's sister is your type, a cool beauty."

"Come on, Maori, don't write that down."

I would love to see this mysterious sister, but it sounds tough with crowds like that.

We take the subway for fifteen minutes to the aquarium. It's the first time I've gone since junior high, and the first time with Izumi. She asks if I want to have our bento right away, but we decide to walk around before we eat. We take turns carrying the basket as we check out the exhibits and fish.

Is there any meaning in memories that are forgotten and never accumulate?

For a second, that negative thought bubbles up, but the colorful fish bring me back to a more innocent state of mind. I feel like they're washing my heart clean.

"Oh, there it is!" Izumi suddenly exclaims. She's looking at a gray creature flapping its wings like an underwater bird.

"I didn't know you liked stingrays, Izumi."

"I do. I've never told you, but I love them."

I thought about making a joke but decided against it when I saw how serious she looked. Instead, I ask her what she liked about them.

"They're the gentlemen of the ocean. They swim so gracefully," she answers succinctly, then presses her nose to the glass like a little kid.

After a minute, she mumbles, "Though, I've gotta wonder what kind of fathers they make. They remind me a little of my dad."

I adore Izumi. She acts like nothing is wrong with me, but I know it can't be easy to have a best friend with amnesia. In my journal, it says she's told me, "I only do what I can do and what I want to do" and "I'm doing this because I like doing it. If I stop liking it, I'll stop doing it. Simple as that." That eases my worry. She was probably considering my mental state when she said it. She's beautiful inside and out.

We do a quick tour of the exhibits and then head to the courtyard. We sit on a bench to eat the lunch my boyfriend made for us. The basket is fairly heavy with food for three. He was carrying it around like it was nothing. What a manly guy.

We take a look at the contents.

"Wow, Kamiya went over the top," Izumi says.

"He really did. This looks even better than last week's. I'm gonna take a picture."

The main dish is *chirashizushi*. It's colorful and, like him, neatly organized. There are perfectly cooked golden strips of egg and a side dish of marinated tuna that looks like something you'd buy. Japanese mustard spinach with sesame seeds balances out the meal. He's included serving chopsticks and paper plates, too.

We take a picture together, then dig in. The vinegared rice has tons of toppings scattered over it that fill my mouth with delicate harmony, and it makes eating a joy.

Izumi sends my boyfriend the photo and a message, but he doesn't respond.

There's a thermos in the basket. When we pour the contents into cups, a fruity fragrance tickles my nose. It's probably Lady Grey.

"I feel like I remember this smell," I mutter. Izumi sinks into thought.

"Memory and smell… Interesting. So you can remember that?"

"I'm not sure if the memory is from when he made it or from some earlier time."

The *chirashizushi* is delicious, and we're both hungry, so we decide to finish it. We're having a good time chatting and eating. Afterward, we drink some more tea.

Suddenly, I hear a kid's happy voice. I look over and see a child pulling her mother's sleeve. The father watches them with a smile.

"In ten years or a little more, everyone will probably be married," I blurt out, still watching the family. I can feel Izumi's eyes on me.

"I wonder…if I'll have a family, too," I say.

"What made you think of that all of a sudden?"

"I'm sorry. I just felt a little afraid, wondering if I'll ever get better."

I smile awkwardly. Izumi looks quietly at the sky.

"I don't think I'll ever get married. I don't think I can. Let's just enjoy things as they come," she says nonchalantly, probably out of consideration for me.

I don't think what she said is true, though. Lots of people have secret crushes on her, both guys and girls. Even though she interacts with people on a surface level, she doesn't open up easily. I wonder if it has something to do with the fact that her parents are separated. I make a joke to cover up my serious thoughts.

"When you say enjoy things, do you mean with me, the girl who will forever feel like a high school student?"

"I've never heard that joke before. Nice one."

"Thanks for sticking with me, Izumi."

"I told you, you don't need to thank me."

"That's right, you're doing this because you like doing it. If you stop liking it, you'll stop doing it."

"What kind of a line is that?! Whoever said it must be twisted."

By the time my boyfriend responds to Izumi's message and meets up with us, it's late afternoon.

"I'm so sorry I broke our promise today," he says when we met him at a bench outside the aquarium.

I gaze at him intently for the first time. His breath is ragged. He must have run here from the station.

"You didn't have to run," I say.

"Hino, seriously, I'm sorry. And Wataya, too," he answers, his breath calmer now.

Izumi watches him silently. Finally, she sighs with resignation.

"Fine. I'm a kind person, so I'll forgive you."

"I'm not a kind person, so I'll ask for a rain check," I joke. My boyfriend smiles kindly.

"You've got it. Let's try the amusement park next time we're all free. I'll pay for half your ticket."

I'm so happy about the idea of going to an amusement park that I don't even worry about him paying for us.

"What a generous boyfriend!" I say.

"Very like you to offer to pay half," Izumi says. "But you don't have to pay for us."

My parents get worried when I'm out late, so the three of us head for the subway.

"Oh, I forgot to tell you. The bento was amazing! Thank you!"

I give him the basket. He takes it with a slightly vacant smile.

The three of us chat happily all the way home. Even though I only talk with him for a little while, I feel strangely at peace and relaxed.

8

The café the woman in the suit named was on the top floor of the mall. I was shown to a window seat overlooking downtown. I'd never been to a place like this before. While I waited nervously for my sister, I ordered some tea and started reading the copy of her book the woman had given me. I'd read it before in a magazine.

However, my mind was too full of thoughts and emotions—about my sister, about telling Wataya I knew about Hino's condition, about leaving my date with Hino—for me to lose myself in the world of the novel. I tried anyway and eventually managed to focus.

How much time had passed? I lost track. When I looked up, my sister was sitting across from me.

"Tooru, have you lost weight?"

To me, she was a pithy, graceful, warm presence. She was wearing a simple but elegant blue shirt that complemented her long black hair nicely.

I didn't know what to say back. She'd spoken so naturally to me after all this time. I smiled, on the verge of tears, and answered as casually as I could.

"I'm not sure. I don't weigh myself very often. I think I grew a bit, though."

"I see. There's a little something I've been wanting to say. Do you mind?"

She usually keeps a straight face, but suddenly, she smiled. It's typical of her to give an introductory comment like that.

"Of course not."

"You've grown so much in the short time I was away. Although, I see you still lose yourself in books just like you used to."

I smiled awkwardly. My chest tightened at her familiar way of speaking. She talks like a character in an old book. Very naturally, too, so it doesn't sound strange. It had been a long time.

"You seem the same yourself," I said.

"Yes."

She must have just arrived, because she ordered tea from a waiter. We hadn't seen each other for a year and a half, but it felt natural, as if we'd only parted yesterday.

"Was it a coincidence? That you were at the bookstore."

It was, but I stumbled over how to answer.

"Yes. Today, I…had something to do. I had some extra time, so I thought I'd stop at the bookstore. I was surprised to find that Keiko Nishikawa was signing books."

"Is that so? And where were you planning to go with the rattan basket?"

I floundered under her teasing look.

"Nothing special. Just meeting a friend from school. It's fine."

"A girl?"

"Uh…yeah."

"You've grown up, Tooru. Are you sure it's fine? I'm sorry for making you wait and, on top of that, cancel your plans."

"Don't worry about it. I wanted to talk to you. Anyway, about your book…," I said, changing the subject. It was my own decision to accept her invitation.

She told me that just having "Akutagawa Prize Nominee" on the cover sent sales soaring, so a rush first edition was printed. People started talking about it online, and an unexpected huge crowd showed up for the signing.

"Huh. That's incredible. I was so happy when I saw in the magazine that it was nominated. You've almost achieved your dream," I said emotionally. She smiled faintly.

"Don't be hasty. I haven't won the prize yet. Anyhow, the important thing is to keep writing. Most people who win the prize can't follow it up. I've made up my mind to make my living as an author, so writing is more important than prizes."

She paused to take a breath.

"I sacrificed my family for it. I sacrificed you," she said with a hint of self-mockery. I didn't know how to respond.

Our mother had always been frail, and when she died of heart disease, my sister took on all the housework. She was only in her first year of junior high. Dad was depressed from losing Mom, and I had only just started first grade. I was worse than useless; I was a burden.

My sister never rested when she was at home. She was constantly cleaning, doing laundry, cooking, taking out the garbage, and caring for me. Her only pleasure was reading novels when all the housework was done. Dad had wanted to be a writer since he was young, so our house was full of old books that my sister ended up reading. I remember her saying to me once, "For me, books are more like places I visit than things I read."

I don't know exactly when she started writing novels. I just knew that on nights when Dad and I fell asleep early, she would secretly write. When she was in her third year of junior high, one of her stories won honorable mention in a local writing contest. Despite that, my sister refused to tell Dad about it. My guess is she didn't want to upset him when he had just started to get back on his feet after Mom's death.

Dad is a hopelessly weak person, but he managed to find some meaning in his life through writing.

My sister kept writing through high school. After graduating, she got an office job with a company that manufactured car parts. She'd wanted to get a government job, but several years passed with none of the nearby municipalities posting a position that only required a high school degree. The factory was her only option.

She helped Dad pay the bills. She had less time to write, but she kept at it. She secretly submitted a manuscript to the New Author Award that Dad was still pining after and made it to the final round. That prize is considered the gateway to the Akutagawa Prize. It was extremely rare for a teenager to make it that far. It was truly an incredible achievement.

She didn't end up winning, but the editor overseeing the contest took an interest in her. They gave her a lot of advice, but she hardly had time to write. She woke up early in the morning to do chores, went to work in the afternoon, and made dinner when she came home at night. Add in more chores and the time spent with Dad, and she didn't even have an hour a day to write. Even though she was working, she stayed as conscientious as ever about housework.

"Mom asked me to do it, and anyway, writing novels isn't really necessary," she would say. On her days off, she collapsed from exhaustion.

When she woke up, she did chores and sometimes went to the library, where she probably wrote.

I'm six years younger than her. At the time, I had finished the first half of my first year of junior high. I had club activities, but I could still help out a little. I knew she was on the verge of giving up on being a writer. Once, when Dad was gone, I heard her fighting with the editor over the phone. I couldn't believe it. My sister? Yelling back emotionally at someone over the phone? "Just because I have talent doesn't mean I can be a burden on my family," she shouted. I remember very clearly how she looked from behind after she hung up. She was looking down, holding both her elbows. She looked like she had lost hope in life.

"Keep writing," I said. Her small frame flinched. She turned toward me slowly.

"Tooru…no. I'm done."

I could tell from her voice that she was trying to give up but couldn't bring herself to cut it off completely.

"That's not good," I said. "I can help with the housework. I'll learn little by little."

"It's fine, really."

"It's not."

"What's gotten into you, Tooru?"

"When I do something bad, you scold me, and I'm grateful for it. So I'm scolding you. Don't give up that easily. I'm begging you. It's your dream, isn't it? To become a novelist?"

She stared at me silently. I went on, desperate to convince her.

"You don't need to stay in this house. I can take care of Dad."

If I've done anything praiseworthy with this insignificant life of mine, it's saying those words. Unfortunately, I was still only six months out of elementary school. I tried not to cry, but my eyes grew hot anyway, and tears spilled down my cheeks. The truth is, I was terrified of what would happen if my sister left. But I wanted to support her anyway.

She looked down, hesitating, then looked back up at me.

"All right. Let's work on it together. I won't quit writing…okay?"

From then on, I started learning how to keep house and cook from her. How to value and strive to be sanitary. That was a pillar of housework for her. Every night at six, when I got home after club activities, I helped her. She was busy with work, and when I'd learned enough, I started leaving club early to shop on my way home and cook dinner. I would wash the bathtub, too. When Dad got home from his job, I would serve him dinner and get his bath ready, like it was nothing. I used to wait proudly for her to come home.

After a year, learning from her and on my own, I basically knew how to run the household. My sister's burden was eased. She had time to rest and write. We only had one computer, and it was Dad's. She used a computer at work, but she wrote her novels by hand back then. I would study while she wrote.

One day in late winter, I learned that I'd gotten into the high school I was aiming for. Early that morning, my sister was bustling around. Dad was still sleeping. At the time, he and I shared a room. I learned later that my sister had been preparing to quit her job since the beginning of my third year of junior high. I lay in the futon next to Dad, staring at the ceiling. I realized she was leaving. I slipped out of bed, taking care not to wake him up, and found her putting her shoes on in the entryway.

"You're going?" I asked.

She stood up. She turned and looked at me with her clear eyes.

"Tooru…"

I wasn't a child anymore when tears would pour down my cheeks even if I tried to resist them. I said the words a person should say when they see someone off.

"I'll see you when you come back."

She picked up her bag.

"Yes. I'll see you when I get back. I'm sorry… I really am."

"I'm sorry for stealing your time and your opportunities for so long."

"You didn't. I know this might make your life harder."

"It's nothing compared to what you did starting from your first year of junior high. Be well, Keiko Nishikawa. I'm rooting for you. I always will be."

"Thank you, Tooru."

That day, she flew off from our familiar apartment complex into the world. About six months later, a novel by Keiko Nishikawa won the *Literary World* New Author Prize. A year and a half later, another book by Nishikawa was nominated for the Akutagawa Prize.

Just in a year and a half. I wanted to reject the word *sacrificed* that she had used.

"I don't feel like I've been abandoned. You couldn't do what you wanted for a long time. You finally did it, and I'm happy. Congratulations. I mean it."

She had been looking down like she was ashamed of herself, but now she looked up. She hesitated for a moment, then smiled calmly.

"Thank you. You're a bit thin, but you look happy. I was planning to get in touch after the Akutagawa Prize was announced, whether I won or not."

"You're not going to see Dad today?"

"I think it would be better not to. Things are still too uncertain."

Suddenly, I remembered how Dad looked when he was writing. He had tried to become a novelist, and she had become one. But he didn't know that.

"Is Dad still trying to become a writer?" she asked a little worriedly. I felt like she'd read my mind.

"Yeah. He's writing something all the time. Sometimes he skips work for it. But enough about that. I want to hear about you."

I tried not to think about him as we talked about all sorts of things. Mostly, I asked her questions. After she left home, she got a job at a bookstore in Tokyo and devoted herself to writing. The woman at the signing was her editor, the same one who had seen her potential from the start.

"What about you? It sounds like you found someone you like."

"Me?"

I thought about what had changed in the past year and a half, and what had not. Images of Hino's innocent laughter and gestures, and of her face as she gazed intently at me, passed through my mind. They only appeared for a moment in the flow of our conversation, but my sister must have seen something in my expression, because she smiled warmly.

Hino was becoming more important to me than my sister. No, not more but equally important. I sensed that quietly and painfully.

"I'm...seeing someone. I mean, we're really more like friends."

"Are you? That sounds like a good thing."

She looked like she already knew. But the next moment, her expression changed to one of surprise.

"She has anterograde amnesia. When she goes to sleep and her brain starts to process her memories, all the memories from that day are erased."

My sister was quiet for a few moments. Who could expect to hear something like that? That their little brother was dating someone with that kind of condition? But she took it seriously.

"And you like her a lot, this girl? Truly, from your heart?"

"Yes. I want to make every day happy for her. I want to enjoy life together. She keeps a daily journal, and I want to fill it with fun things so that every day, when she reads it, she'll feel a little more optimistic about her life."

My sister closed her eyes. When she opened them, they were full of warmth.

"Thank you for telling me. This might sound a bit dramatic, but I wish the two of you all the happiness in the world."

"Thank you."

She smiled faintly. Then she took out a phone, which she'd never had when she lived at home, and pulled up her own number.

"I need to have a phone now. Can we exchange numbers?"

I pulled out my own phone, hesitated for a moment, then added her as "Keiko Nishikawa." She typed in my number and, still holding her phone, looked down.

"I feel so bad to have left Dad entirely in your hands. If you ever have trouble with him, please don't hesitate to call me."

"Thanks. But this is the most important time for you. We're fine. Don't worry about us," I said confidently.

"You've become quite the shoulder to lean on," she said, smiling.

I smiled back.

"But I'm glad," she went on. "I'm glad you have someone you care about. Her amnesia might not be cured easily, but make sure you treat her the best you can."

She was looking at me with gentle eyes. Kindness and warmth felt as natural as air and water when I was with my sister. I hoped that memory, that sensation would carry over in my relationships with other people, even a little.

"I will. And I won't just treat her well. I'll do everything I can to be that kind of person."

I stood and reached for the bill. My sister blocked my hand.

"I'll get this one," she said.

"You sure? Thanks."

"You're welcome. I'm coming to a turning point soon. Until then, take good care of Dad."

We left the café together and met up with the editor, who was waiting in the hotel lobby on the first floor. She said my sister had a signing the next day in a different city. My sister and I both managed a smile and said our goodbyes.

I took out my phone and responded to Wataya's message that I'd seen when I was exchanging numbers with my sister. I said I'd meet her and Hino on a bench outside the aquarium. I took the subway to the nearest stop and walked from there under the twilight sky. Everyone had problems. However, right then, in that moment, I felt all of them fade away within me. I wasn't a powerless child anymore. I was still a kid, but I was past the age when I couldn't do anything. At the very least, I could walk with my own two feet.

There was someone I wanted to see. And I could reach her side on my own feet.

Partway there, I couldn't contain myself. I took off running. Hino's face was all I could think of. My whole body was filled with joy. Maybe because I was running, my heart started beating, and for a second, it tightened painfully. I stumbled but managed not to fall. Maybe it was because I was running on an empty stomach. I laughed at my own ridiculousness. But that was me, and it was okay. Each step connected me to her.

I started sprinting again. It was the powerful urge I had been waiting for.

9

I had been dating Hino for three weeks. Finals were almost here. We were in the library together after school.

As long as she was a student, she couldn't avoid tests. But it was impossible for her to retain new information. Her memories only lasted a single day. I thought about that as I watched her, bent over her notebook, scribbling something.

"What's wrong, Tooru?" she asked, noticing my gaze and looking up.

"Nothing, you just seem calmer than usual."

"I'm not going to get rowdy around the library."

"Who cares? Why not?"

"Come on, stop. You're kind of…making me want to," she said shyly.

I smiled at her. Earlier, in my classroom, I'd asked her what she wanted to do today. She'd said she wanted to study together. It was one of the things she'd mentioned wanting to do before. We headed to the library and sat down across from each other at a table. That much was fine. But she kept glancing at me, and she clearly wasn't writing words in her notebook. Her textbook wasn't even open.

Growing suddenly suspicious, I leaned over the table and took a peek at her notebook.

"Hey! Stop!" she said, flustered.

On the page was a picture of an average-looking teenage boy with no outstanding features whatsoever. In other words, me.

"You sure must be on top of your schoolwork," I said, sitting back down.

"Resting is important, too!" she said, smiling to throw me off.

"We haven't exactly done enough to need a break," I answered.

"Hey, did my boyfriend just say something suggestive?"

"No, I mean…you're really good at drawing."

I was partly trying to change the subject but also genuinely surprised. Although I'd only gotten a glance, her drawing skills were better than average. She must have taken classes.

"Why are you so good?" I asked.

"Am I?" she answered, sounding pleased. "I guess I never told you. I was in art club in junior high. I even won some prizes."

"That doesn't sound like you."

"Hey, that was rude!"

"Kidding."

"I know."

We exchanged smiles, and she let me see her drawing. I felt embarrassed, but more than that, impressed. I guess you'd call it a portrait. I could definitely tell she'd studied art. It was way beyond what I could do.

"I quit when I started high school, but all of a sudden, I felt like drawing you."

"Huh. Art. Interesting…"

The Sunday after our botched aquarium date, it had suddenly occurred to me to do some research on Hino's amnesia. While my dad was on a walk, taking a break from writing, I borrowed the computer to search online.

I found out that there are basically two types of memory, short-term and long-term. Short-term memory is the kind you only retain for a little while, like remembering a phone number long enough to call it. Long-term memory refers to things that you recall multiple times so you won't forget, like if you're studying for a test, and those things become established memories. If you have anterograde amnesia, you can't create new long-term memories, but it doesn't mean you lose all your previous ones.

To get further into the weeds, there are two types of long-term memory, declarative and procedural. Declarative memory involves conscious recollection, where you can write down information, including factual things like what you did yesterday. This is usually what people are referring to when they talk about memories.

But that day, when we were studying together, I was thinking about procedural memory. That's the kind you can't write down, like, to give a simple example, how to ride a bike. Most of knowing how to ride a bike involves sensations. Even if you lost a day of memories, you wouldn't lose your muscle memory, the ones rooted in your body rather than in your brain.

I didn't look into the details, but my guess was that drawing might be a procedural memory. I felt like I'd discovered something. I handed Hino's notebook back and said, trying to hide my excitement, "It's cool that you have a special skill or hobby like that."

"You think so? But I'm really not that good," she said modestly. Still, she seemed happy.

"I'm jealous. My only hobby is reading. I bet something like drawing is like riding a bike. Once you learn, you don't easily forget it."

"What? Oh, right. I wonder."

She looked at me blankly. Pretending to show off my random knowledge, I told her about short-term and long-term memories. I explained that, while knowledge is important for drawing, it must also have a lot to do with procedural memories, or the body's sense for how to do things. The more you draw, the better you get. Your body remembers how to do it.

After I finished talking, Hino looked lost in thought.

"Hino, are you okay?" I asked, a little worried.

"Oh, yeah, I'm fine. Sorry. I was just thinking. Procedural memory, that's interesting."

She sank into thought again.

"You think procedural memories don't go away?" she suddenly asked.

"I wonder if people with amnesia forget how to ride a bike," I said, knowing I was taking a fairly big risk.

"I don't think so," she said.

"Then there's your answer."

"Huh."

"Yeah."

"Interesting."

The next instant, her brooding expression crumpled into a smile. *Crumple* really is the right word for it. To me, it looked like she was trying to hide her happiness and not quite succeeding.

We didn't do much of anything for the rest of the day. I completed some worksheets we had for homework, and Hino kept drawing in her notebook.

On the way home, I asked her, "Was today okay? We didn't do anything very fun."

"What? No, it was fine! I learned something pretty important, and I had fun drawing you."

Something pretty important.

I'd mentioned it casually, but I was hoping it might improve her everyday life in some small way. If she got in the habit of drawing, each day's version of herself might enjoy life a little more. Ultimately, people draw the greatest strength from within themselves.

"Honestly, I wish you wouldn't draw me anymore," I said, trying to sound casual despite my serious thoughts. "It's embarrassing. How about drawing Wataya instead? She's got nice facial features."

Hino struck a thinker's pose.

"In other words, my boyfriend thinks Wataya has a pretty face?"

"I didn't say that!"

She teased me about that for the rest of the day.

The next day, I noticed something. Hino seemed to be influenced by her most recent journal entries.

Once again, she said she wanted to study together in the library and spent the time drawing me. The rest of the week passed uneventfully, and then our exams came. Hino sat for finals, but her grades didn't matter.

During test week, we studied with Wataya, and each time, Hino drew me, although she tried to hide it. Wataya knew she'd started drawing. She also seemed to have heard that it was me who suggested it. The previous week, when I was switching rooms for one of my classes, someone slapped me hard on the back. I highly doubt many people would realize that was her way of expressing appreciation. I looked over and saw her smiling at me meaningfully, her hand still on my back.

"So why are you hiding the fact that you know about her amnesia?" she asked.

Hino wasn't there, so I doubt she knew Wataya was bringing it up with me.

"Hino's trying to keep it secret, and I don't see any point in letting on that I know," I answered.

She looked at me skeptically, as if she was weighing my words. When I thought about it, I realized this was an opportunity. I made up my mind and said, "Actually, Hino told me why she keeps her amnesia a secret from the kids at school."

Wataya made a surprised noise but didn't say anything else.

"I could sense her anxiety and fear," I went on. "I mean, it's scary, right? There are bad people in the world. I bet a fair number of jerks would come out of the woodwork thinking they could do anything to her because she wouldn't remember it. It's the perfect situation for bullying or abuse. She'd forget it all."

Wataya stiffened nervously.

"You're not like that, right? You wouldn't do anything like that to her?"

"Of course not. But my class doesn't have a very good reputation. We've had some harassment incidents. If she knew her boyfriend was in that class, and he knew about her amnesia…what would she think every day? I bet she'd be worried."

I didn't know what she'd written in her notebooks about my personality or our relationship. Though, I'm willing to bet she'd written down that I told her I liked her as part of a bullying incident. Wataya didn't know that part, but it could add to Hino's anxiety.

"So that's why you aren't telling her?"

"Right."

The truth was, I wished I could support Hino in the same way Wataya did, as someone who knew about her amnesia. However, Hino and I hadn't even known each other before this. Even though we spent every day together after school, there was a crucial difference. From her perspective, we'd never met.

I was thinking about that distance I could never bridge when Wataya said, "I thought you two would break up right away. Actually, I still think you will."

Her words could be seen as harsh, but suddenly she smiled.

"But…yeah. After what you said just now, I feel like I understand you a little better. I'm glad you're a good guy. But don't you think you're taking on too much? Make sure you don't burn out and keel over one day."

I wasn't sure if she was joking, so I smiled vaguely.

"If that happens, I'll leave the rest in your hands."

"Me? Take over for you? Well, I do feel like I could play a guy's role in the all-female theater troupe Takarazuka Revue."

"Hino might be the man in our relationship."

"I don't want to see you in a frilly dress."

After that, we made a point of not talking about serious things. We agreed to only contact each other if we were really in trouble and to act normal in front of Hino.

When Hino tried to draw Wataya's portrait while we studied in the library after school one day, Wataya teased her.

"I don't care if you draw me, Maori, but can you please stop drawing me with a frown on your face?"

"I was just noticing how perfect your facial features are. Damn you…!"

"What did I ever do to you? Hey, boyfriend, say something!" Wataya said, pulling me in.

"I think your features are perfect, too, Hino," I said casually.

"What, really? Are you falling for me?"

"Yes, I love you!"

"Oh, I'm so happy!"

"You two sound like bad actors reading a script."

Sometimes, in the middle of all this, it would hit me.

I was taking our school routine for granted, but summer vacation was coming. What would happen to Hino then? She would wake up in the morning and learn she had amnesia. She'd read her notebooks and gradually accept her situation. But there would be no school.

With time on her hands and the sun shining down, how would she feel?

At the very least, it would be good if she had a hobby to entertain her. If she decided on a theme, she might be able to work on her drawings across many days, passing them from one self to the next.

Wouldn't it be great if she could accomplish something even in her current state?

I'd wanted to take Hino to the amusement park on Saturday, but I had to put it off because of finals. That made two weeks in a row that I hadn't been able to keep my promise. The previous weekend, she had some things to do, while I had jobs to do for the neighborhood association at my apartment complex. She didn't tell me exactly what she had to do, but she probably has checkups or tests at the hospital once a month.

Now it was July. Our finals spanned over five consecutive days. During that testing period, the three of us went to the library together, and once again Hino started furtively drawing me in her sketchbook, peering at me curiously as she did. I felt restless, but I served as a model without complaint.

Tests ended, and Saturday finally arrived. The three of us went to the amusement park. Hino and Wataya made me go on the roller coaster three times in a row. I'd never been to a theme park, and I realized what a terrifying place it is. I must have looked like I was suffering, because Hino kept asking me if I was all right, like she felt sorry for me. At one point, I said something weird when I answered.

"Oh, I'm fine," I said. "Don't worry about me. I like doing new things with you. I'm always trying to think of ways for you to have fun."

The two of them gave me an awkward look.

"What? What's wrong?" I asked, panicking a little.

Wataya scratched her cheek uncomfortably.

"Nothing, it's just…sometimes you give these embarrassing little speeches."

I started blushing and changed the subject by suggesting we have a late lunch. After we ate, we walked around the grounds. As the sky turned orange, we talked about summer vacation. I suspected Wataya would start studying for college entrance exams since she's in the advanced class, but she didn't bring it up. She was probably being considerate of Hino. Instead, she grumbled that she'd have to spend the whole time helping her mom and reading. I said I'd probably be doing the same thing, since I don't have any hobbies.

"Are you going to draw and stuff?" I asked. Hino hadn't said anything so far. She nodded.

"Summer…," she mumbled.

To her, yesterday was spring, but when she woke up, it was suddenly summer. The word *surprised* didn't begin to express it. I think it must have been a sad feeling.

"I'm jealous of you two," Wataya sighed, filling in the silence between Hino and me. "You have each other, and you can go on as many dates as you want."

"Let's hang out together and go to lots of places," I answered. "We can go to some festivals and set off fireworks. Let's live it up."

Sometimes, twilight brings melancholy along with darkness. I was trying to brighten up the mood. Hino stopped walking and turned to me with a distant look in her eyes.

"Yes, that sounds nice."

She smiled faintly.

Summer was just around the corner.

Once-in-a-Lifetime
Summer

1

Morning at home: as usual

Afternoon at home: Drawing. Thought about setting a goal for how many drawings I should finish over summer break. What will tomorrow's me think? Finished three simple still lifes.

With my boyfriend: I went to the library at four in the afternoon. He was in the study room looking at a reference book. We talked. He said that during breaks from studying, he'd been looking at art books for me. He showed me a few. Not only that, he also summarized the main points for me. He said there are various methods for improving at drawing, but one important technique is to draw quickly. By drawing something as soon as you see it, before you have time to think, your senses are utilized as much as possible. It's called *croquis* in French, mainly applies to things that move, like people.

I thought about that. Sharpening my senses feels like a good approach for me right now. Also, I remember my junior high art teacher talking about the importance of sketching. I decided to start a new section for notes about drawing, so refer to that ("Art" page in the binder).

But I wonder if my boyfriend is falling behind on his own studies because he's helping me so much. I asked him, and he just smiled. It was kinda cute.

Afterward, the two of us went to the stationery store near the library. I bought a pad of paper for sketching. There are more sheets compared to a regular sketchbook, and it's thinner and bigger. My boyfriend Mr. Thrifty paid for it, said it was to celebrate. Next time I'll buy him tea or something. Remember that, my future selves!

The locusts are trilling outside, a sign that it really is summer. It's so hot, I have to keep the air conditioner on all the time, but even then, I'm still covered in sweat.

Time moves on, leaving me behind, alone.

"Earth, stop turning!" I say, then realize that won't do much good and restart the AC.

When I woke up and found out it was summer vacation, I couldn't manage a smile. To make matters worse, I can't retain information anymore.

I look at the middle finger of my right hand. I don't tell other people this, but I like my hands. The callus on that finger is physical proof that I spent hours with a pen in my hand studying every day even after I got into high school. That's how I got into the advanced class in my second year. Except the callus is going away now.

I couldn't work hard anymore. Or, to be more accurate, even if I work hard, I won't get any smarter. It makes me want to cry a little.

Still, in the afternoon, I manage to sort out my thoughts. I've got a handle on my situation and my friends. And it's summer, the season for love.

Even in this state, I have a boyfriend.

On a page in the sketchpad on my desk, there's a portrait of a teenage boy I barely recognize. Apparently, this guy with the oval face is my boyfriend.

There are a lot of other drawings in the book, including some figure drawings. I quit doing art when I started high school so I could concentrate on studying, but it seems that lately, during summer vacation, I've been drawing every day. Maybe that's why my callus hasn't completely disappeared. I got the sketchbook recently, and there's no sign of a huge improvement in the few dozen pages I've filled. Nonetheless, I'm definitely getting better, slowly advancing like a turtle.

It seems my boyfriend has something to do with me starting to draw again. After learning of the technical term "procedural memory," my past selves seem to have concluded that maybe, even now, I could retain these procedural memories, which are like physical memories. In other words, there was a possibility I could improve at drawing.

That turned out to be true. My old pictures serve as a testament. I looked up some more information on the internet and found out that procedural memory is also called implicit memory. Besides drawing, practicing music and other similar things also help develop those memories.

I don't have much to do today, so I read the binder section on "Art" and try out some croquis sketches, a technique that my recent selves have been practicing in my sketchbook.

I play a foreign film on my laptop and stop it at a scene I like, using the actor as my model. Instead of thinking about it, I let my hand do the work, focusing on the sensations I feel while sketching. Just like in junior high, when I was drawing every day, the picture comes together easily. Compared to my first drawings, the lines now look more confident. I must be doing this every day to kill time. I admit, it's fun. My selves from previous days are in those skillful lines.

They offer proof that even now, I can continue and achieve something over time and grow and develop. Knowing that makes me happy.

I sharpen my focus and do another drawing. My phone lights up. It's a message from Izumi.

Hey, how's it going?

I snap a photo of the drawing I'm working on and send it to her. She is amazed.

That's so good! You're really getting better every day.

I've got a long way to go. But it's fun. And it kills a lot of time.

I wish I had some kind of artistic hobby like that.

Now that I think of it, I've never seen you do a drawing. What's your style like?

They'll probably be very popular a few thousand years after I die.

That's not artistic value, that's archaeological value!

If I started counting the amount of bad things about my life right now, I could go on forever. So I try to focus on the good stuff. The best of all is that I already know Izumi. When I chat with her about silly stuff, I feel truly happy and at peace.

By the way, are you meeting up with Kamiya today?

Yeah. We're meeting at the library in the afternoon at four.

Ah, young love.

Izumi, sometimes you sound like an old man.

Based on my journal, it seems I've been seeing my boyfriend almost every day over summer vacation. Recently, he showed me some art books, and before that, he took me to a game center. He won a teddy bear for me to draw, and I was really excited. Yet I can't find it. I guess I put it away somewhere the day I got it. I wrote the reason down. It's a little complicated, but it was that-day's me who wanted him to get the bear for her. The next day, if all that was left was the teddy bear and the fact that my boyfriend got it for me, that me might be confused or unhappy about it. I can be so annoying. Though, I could be right.

After that, I message Izumi some more and go back to sketching. I read the art books from the library, too, reviewing the pages that my past selves read.

I decide to focus on drawing fast today. I set a limit of five minutes per page and start sketching a foreign actor I like. Finishing a drawing in five minutes is hard. Still, if I do it every day, maybe I'll get better. My efforts might add up and have an effect.

Soon, it's after three, so I spritz on some perfume, get myself ready, and ride my bike to the library. The sensation of summer clings to my bare skin.

It's less than ten minutes from my house to the library. From my boyfriend's house, it takes roughly half an hour, but he's kind enough to meet me there every day.

"Oh, there you are! You're actually studying today."

"Hi, Hino. Don't worry; I'm a good student."

I find him in the study room at the library. It's the guy from my sketchbook. According to my binder, he's always in the same position in the same spot, so he's easy to find.

Izumi is going to summer school. She's enrolled in another test-prep place for college entrance exams, too, so she's kind of busy. To tell the truth, if I hadn't started drawing again and if I didn't have a boyfriend, I think my pessimism would have crushed me.

My boyfriend puts away his stuff, and we go down to the break room on the first floor, where there's a vending machine. My boyfriend says he's not planning to go to university. Instead, he's hoping to get a government job at a municipal office that only requires a high school degree, even if he has to commute a long way to get there. That's why he's not too worried about studying.

"Hino, what do you want to do today? You're free till seven, right?"

"Right. Oh, I know! I want to go look at straw hats. It's summer, after all. But you're not allowed to buy me one, okay?"

My boyfriend sulks a little but quickly agrees.

"Okay. I'm useless as a sugar daddy anyway. Is the mall by the train station okay?"

I tell him it is, and we get our bikes from the parking area. As I watch my boyfriend unlock his bike, my eyes fall on the cargo rack.

"Think it's too dangerous to ride together? There are probably police around since we're downtown."

I'd remembered the diary entries about how much fun we had riding a bike together before. He thinks for a minute.

"They might be cracking down since it's summer vacation. But maybe we can do it."

"Really?"

"Let's give it a try."

He grips the handlebar with one hand and kicks up the stand. He tells me to straddle the seat, so I do. He puts his other hand on the handlebar and starts walking. The bike rolls gently along with me on it.

…Huh?

As you can probably imagine, I'm like a princess on the horse, and he's the knight holding the reins. This is mortifying. I name this "princess riding." He doesn't seem to notice anything strange, because he walks right out of the parking lot like that.

"Hey, no, wait!" I say.

"What? I thought we'd go to the mall like this."

Overwhelmed by embarrassment, I cover my face with both hands. I can feel it burning up. Maybe if I'd put on more makeup, I would have felt bolder. But not like this.

"We can't let anyone see us this way!" I protest. Fortunately, we don't run into anyone. He finally seems to realize why I'm so embarrassed, because he suddenly takes his hands off the handlebars. I wobble. I try to put my feet down quickly, but the seat is too high. This is not good. I'm going to fall over with the bicycle!

Just then, my boyfriend wraps his arm around my waist and saves me. He grabs the handlebars with his other hand, and the bike stays upright. To put it simply, I'm now in my boyfriend's arms.

"Oh!"

"Oh…s-sorry!"

He's panicking, but then a giggle escapes my mouth. In this position, my feet can reach the ground, so I manage to pull myself away, feeling his eyes on me all the while. He sets the bike upright as I watch him. I feel laughter bubbling up in my stomach. I try to stop it, but I can't. I clap my hand over my mouth.

"What's wrong, Hino?"

I can't hold it in anymore. I burst out laughing.

"What is this?" I giggle. "This is the worst romantic comedy ever! Ahhh, it's hilarious. I've never seen a couple ride together like that! How can you do that without getting embarrassed?"

My boyfriend scratches his head awkwardly.

"I don't know…I'm sorry. It's just, when you said you were worried about the police catching us, I thought this might work. But you're right, it was weird."

Suddenly, his expression relaxes.

"It definitely was! Catching me when I was about to fall off the bike? That's straight out of a shoujo manga! It's summer. We're high school students. Does this even happen in real life? It's shocking. But more than that, it's hilarious!"

We both start laughing like we're remembering it all over again. Eventually, we each get on our own bike and ride to the mall. Window-shopping is fun enough, so I don't end up buying anything. We get ready to go home.

"Bye, Hino. See you tomorrow," my boyfriend says.

"See you tomorrow."

I watch him ride into the distance. It's weird to say this, but the me of this morning was jealous of the me of yesterday. I felt like it was unfair of my past selves to be having so much fun, according to the diary, while I felt so hopeless. I wanted those enjoyable memories to be my own. I wanted to share in their fun. I wanted to take normal things for granted, like I always did before.

After hanging out with my boyfriend, though, those ugly feelings have gone away. I sympathize with yesterday's me, because she also felt like I do now when she wrote in the diary. That's another weird thing to say—that I sympathize with yesterday's me.

Oddly enough, when I saw my boyfriend, who should have been a stranger to me, my heart throbbed a little. I can't store information, but maybe other things do stay with me. Emotions, feelings.

For one, I think I'm starting to like him. No, that can't be possible. But…maybe it is.

I watched him as we were shopping. He wore a troubled smile.

I think about it on the way home. I have dinner and take a bath. I write in my diary, and in the short time before going to bed, I sketch. I draw the scene I'm thinking about: when my boyfriend was pushing me on the bike. I'm not in a bad mood as I draw.

2

On August 12, the winners of the Akutagawa Prize and the Naoki Prize for the first half of the year are announced.

I was restless from the time I woke up. Dad must have felt the same way, because he seemed on edge since the morning. He still didn't know that Keiko Nishikawa was his own daughter. Still, he had his eye on the Akutagawa Prize, and not just because he likes literature. As an aspiring novelist, I think he feels a mixture of longing and regret and even something like envy.

After he left for work, I packed a simple lunch and headed to the library as usual. I brought a little radio with me. The prizewinner would probably be posted online first, but the radio news would announce it, too.

By noon, they still hadn't announced it yet. I like literature, but I don't listen for the winner in real time like this every year. I usually find out in the next day's paper, so I didn't know what time they would announce it.

I ate my lunch and then went to the magazine rack to search for the issue with Keiko Nishikawa's nominated story in it. I read it over again from the start. I don't know how many times I did.

Two o'clock passed before I knew it. As I was about to turn on the radio, someone approached me.

"Excuse me…"

"Hino?"

I looked up at the sound of her familiar voice. This was different from our usual routine.

"What's wrong? It's not four yet, is it?"

She was standing nervously in front of me, wearing a white dress that made her look a bit like a girl from some wealthy family and holding a big straw hat in both hands.

"No, but you'll find out about your sister today, right? Would you mind if I waited with you? We'll be able to hear the news immediately on my phone, and I think we'll be able to watch the live conference."

I hadn't told yesterday's Hino that today was the Akutagawa Prize announcement. She must have looked it up herself. Or maybe Wataya told her.

I nodded, put the magazine back, and, at Hino's suggestion, went with her to the break room. On the way, I noticed the straw hat again.

"That one did look good on you," I said. It was the one we'd seen the day before at the mall near the station. Hino had been trying to decide between two styles, and she must have gone back to buy the one I said looked better. I'd wanted to get it for her, but maybe she beat me to it on purpose so I didn't have to spend the money. That sounded like her. However, for some reason, when I mentioned it, she seemed upset.

"What? You recognize this hat?"

"What?"

I thought about what she'd said. She'd forgotten we saw it together. I thought back over the happy memories from the day before. There was the embarrassing episode in the parking lot. Afterward, we went window-shopping. She'd messed around, putting the women's straw hat on me. We'd both laughed about it. To me, it was an important memory, but she didn't remember it. To her...that was normal. She forgot everything.

"I wanted to go to the big art store by the station, so I got my mom to drive me there this morning," she said. "I stopped into some shops on the way, and I just loved this one from the moment I saw it, so..."

She seemed to be having trouble explaining. I flashed a desperate smile. Not only had she gone out that morning, but she'd also met me earlier than usual. She probably hadn't planned on that. It couldn't be helped. Reading all her diary entries must take a long time.

"Ah, gotcha. It's nothing important. I just remembered you glanced at it when we went to the mall together, so I was wondering about it. I guess it's not good to be overly observant, huh?" I said, trying to brush it off by stringing together some things I wouldn't usually say. I didn't mention the fact that I'd considered selling some used books to get the money to buy the hat for her.

Hino looked slightly uncomfortable, but when I told her how good it looked, she returned to acting like her usual self. Wataya was waiting for us in the break room.

"I thought you might have told her," I said to Wataya, pulling myself together after my interaction with Hino. "Thanks for making the trip down here. You came because you knew they were announcing the Akutagawa Prize today, right?"

"Yup," Wataya answered, looking slightly worried. "Sorry to barge in like this. Are we bothering you?"

"Not at all. To tell the truth, I couldn't concentrate, so I'm glad you're here."

"Okay, that's good. Let's all wait together. I'm kind of on edge myself."

According to her research, the prize was announced at a different time every year, but a live online press conference with the winner was scheduled to start at six. We still had some time, so Hino read my sister's nominated story while Wataya and I sat around restlessly. Wataya said this was her first time watching the announcement live.

"Calm down, you two!" scolded Hino. We'd been getting up and down from our seats and making pointless trips to the washroom.

"We are calm," I insisted. "Completely calm. Right, Wataya?"

"Oh, yes, very. We couldn't care less," she added.

"Really, now?" Hino said.

The clock ticked on. As six o'clock approached, we went outside so we wouldn't bother the other library patrons and watched the online program on Hino's phone.

"The live broadcast of the Akutagawa Prize and the thirty-fifth Naoki Prize winners' press conference will begin shortly," an announcer said.

It was finally starting. Two men were seated at a long table. One was introduced as a commentator and began giving some introductory remarks about the origins of the two prizes. He and the other guy, his assistant, must have been speaking at the venue where the press conference would take place. The tension in the air was apparent on-screen.

Since it was a live broadcast, all the nominees must be waiting in another room. I wondered what my sister was feeling at the moment. Time dragged on with no announcement of the winner. According to the commentator, it probably wasn't going to happen until between seven and eight. That was still an hour or two away. My dad had said he was eating out that night, so I didn't need to cook. I could stay out late, but the library was closing at seven. We needed to go somewhere else. I looked up from the phone at Wataya and Hino.

"What should we do? I wouldn't mind going to a family restaurant or something, but what about your parents? You could go home now if you need to."

"I'm sure my mom wouldn't care. What about you, Maori?" Wataya said right away.

"They won't mind as long as I call and tell them. It's a special thing, so I think we should all wait together. But where should we go? The nearest family restaurant is kind of far away. Izumi is on her bike, and if we get there late, we might miss something."

My house was closer than Wataya's. The streets were still relatively safe during the day, but a summer night could be dangerous.

"Then how about I sleep over at your place, Hino?" Wataya said casually. "Should we sneak Kamiya into your room?"

"What?!" I blurted out loudly. Hino seemed more surprised by my reaction than by Wataya's suggestion.

Hino's house. It was summer vacation and all, but I still felt hesitant about going to a girl's house at night. It wouldn't look very good if her parents caught us.

"Sorry for shouting, but I don't think it's a good idea," I protested. "How about we go to a family restaurant by the station? I know I'm no hulk, but I can walk you back to Wataya's house afterward."

Hino ignored me, lost in thought. Wataya was grinning. Crap!

Hino thought I didn't know about her amnesia. I wasn't sure what she'd told her parents about me, but wouldn't it be a heap of trouble if I went to her house?

Then she smiled like she'd made up her mind and said cheerfully, "Okay! We'll sneak Kamiya into my room, so my parents won't know he's there, and wait for the announcement together. What do you say?"

I froze. If there was any way out of this, I would've liked it if someone told me how. But Wataya jumped in to say she thought it was a great idea, and the two of them started frolicking around like it was all decided.

"Hey, wait…what?" I mumbled.

3

Hino and Wataya basically forced me to go with them to Hino's house. According to Hino, her dad was overprotective, so we came up with a strategy to smuggle me inside. Our plan was that Hino would tell her mom that Wataya was coming over, and the three of us would head to her house. While Wataya chatted with Hino's parents in the living room, Hino would bring me inside, and the two of us would go upstairs to the hallway outside her room. She would clean up her room quickly, and when she was done, I would go in.

When Hino called her mom, she said she'd be happy to have Wataya come over, especially since it was summer vacation. She didn't even mind if she slept over.

"By the way," I said as the three of us rode our bikes toward Hino's house, "how am I supposed to leave?"

"Don't worry," Wataya answered confidently. "I'll chat with them in the living room again. You can just slip out then."

We arrived at Hino's house. It was my first time seeing it, and it wasn't one of those cookie-cutter houses. It was a proper single-family home.

I walked off a little ways and locked up my bike by the side of the road. When I got back and peeked into the yard, I saw the two of them walking into the entryway, waving at Hino's parents. A few minutes later, the front door opened again. Hino poked her face out, obviously enjoying the prank, and gestured for me to come in. I tiptoed into her house.

"Carry your shoes, okay?" she whispered.

"Okay," I replied, picking them up.

I looked over at the closed door that must lead to the living room and heard Wataya's cheerful voice coming from the other side. Hino's parents were in there. I wondered what they were like.

"What are you doing?!" she hissed, bringing me back from the clouds. I followed her. We went upstairs. Apparently, the room at the end of the hallway was hers.

While she cleaned up, I waited anxiously outside.

The door opened, and she gestured for me to come in. Her room was much bigger than mine and very tidy. She told me to put my shoes on top of a magazine she laid out that she planned to throw away, so I did.

"I'll go get Izumi and bring some food back for us. Wait a minute, okay?" she said.

"Okay, sure," I answered.

She closed the door, leaving me alone. I let out a long breath. Then the door opened again, and I jumped. Hino smirked at me.

"This is a girl's room. You may be my boyfriend, but you better not look at my underwear or anything!"

"I w-wouldn't do that."

She gave me a long look.

"You can peek if you want."

"I told you I won't!"

She was definitely teasing me. As I thought about how to make her go away, she stared at me some more.

"Can I ask you a weird question?" she inquired.

"No way. Don't ask anything too awkward in this situation."

"Do you like me, Tooru?"

"What…?"

For a second, I forgot about all my complicated emotions. The ticking of the clock thundered in my ears.

"Why are you asking me that? Did you forget the third condition?"

I had no idea what to say. I smiled, trying to keep myself from sounding too serious, but I didn't know if it worked.

"Oh, I remember. But…I was just wondering, and I wanted to ask you."

"Don't worry. I won't really fall in love with you," I reassured her.

There was no way I could admit I'd fallen in love with her a long time ago. I made an effort to curl my lips into a tense half smile.

"Oh… Okay. Sorry for the weird question," she mumbled. Maybe I was imagining it, but her smile looked a little sad.

"It's fine. But it's not like you to wonder about something like that. What's up?" I asked.

She smiled playfully, making me think I'd misread her expression a moment ago.

"Nothing. I was just thinking that if you really liked me, I'd better be prepared to lose a pair or two of panties."

"I told you I'd never do that!" I accidentally shouted, then slapped my hand over my mouth.

"Enjoy your time," Hino said, smiling as she closed the door. I heard her footsteps fade and let out another long breath.

I won't really fall in love with you. Really?

If the world were different, what would our relationship be like? Would I keep hiding my feelings for her while she kept her amnesia a secret and continued our fake romance?

It wouldn't last long. I felt like we would break up eventually. I smiled bitterly at having thought that. I didn't regret falling for her. Even if my feelings came to nothing…I didn't care.

I closed my eyes, trying to switch gears. But what should I do? I had some time before the two of them came back. I opened my eyes and looked around Hino's room.

Ogling a girl's room was definitely bad. But I noticed the sketchbook we'd bought together lying on her desk. I walked over to it. There was a pencil next to it, along with a sharpener and a small utility knife. It smelled a little like the art room in junior high.

I knew it was wrong, but I wanted to know more about Hino, so I flipped through the notebook. There were several line drawings of people. Suddenly, my own face appeared, and my hand stopped.

The me in her sketchbook had a troubled smile on his face. I vaguely remembered making an expression like that in a photo she took earlier during vacation.

I flipped the page. There were more sketches of me smiling pitifully or looking away. Other drawings weren't fleshed out yet. I recognized a few of the poses. One looked like me from behind, pushing Hino on her bike in the library parking lot. I wondered how she thought of me.

What, you recognize this hat?

I remembered our exchange about the hat with a twinge of pain, but I tried to ignore it. Slowly, I closed the sketchbook. I noticed a piece of paper poking out of the wide drawer of her desk. What was it? She'd said she wanted to clean up before I came in. Maybe it had something to do with that.

I hesitated, but when would I have another chance like this? My hand reached out.

There were several pieces of paper in the drawer, along with a binder and notebooks. Written on the piece of paper, in Hino's handwriting: *I've suffered memory loss in an accident. Read the notebook on the desk.*

I quickly closed the drawer. Noticing that the paper was still sticking out, I quickly arranged it so it wouldn't crease.

My heart was pounding, and my hands were shaking.

Cruelty lurked beneath the surface of life. That thought suddenly crossed my mind. People might not notice it, but cruelty was hiding all over the place.

Hino had told me about the binder and notebooks that day at the park, but she hadn't mentioned the pieces of paper. She probably hung them on the wall where she would see them every day.

Every day, she was forced to face her illness. I felt like I'd glimpsed the reality of her life that I'd been so terrified of. The reality she tried so hard to keep from me. She always smiled, no matter what. I, on the other hand…

Hearing two sets of footsteps approaching, I stiffened. I had to pretend I was doing something else. I grabbed an art book lying nearby.

"Have you been a good boy? Oh, look, you're reading a book. Typical," Hino said with a mixture of exasperation and admiration.

"Kamiya, why aren't you acting more like a typical boyfriend?" Wataya asked, following Hino into the room.

"What do you mean, 'typical'?"

"You know, wearing Maori's underwear on your head or stuffing a bra in your pocket with the strap hanging out or something."

"Strap? Honestly, just stop."

I let out a quiet sigh of relief that for now they didn't seem suspicious. Hino set the tray she was carrying down on a low table. There were two plates of curry and rice, one with a huge serving and the other normal. There were two spoons and two cups as well.

"I brought us dinner so we don't get hungry. Izumi and I will share the big plate; you can have the smaller one," Hino said.

"Nice. Thanks."

We stuffed ourselves with the spicy curry and watched the live coverage on Hino's laptop. Instead of the commentator, the screen now showed a big room at what looked like some fancy hotel. A whiteboard was set in the center of a low stage.

Two pieces of paper were taped to the whiteboard. One read *Akutagawa Prize*, the other *Naoki Prize*. What I guessed were reporters sat in chairs facing the stage, glancing at the whiteboard periodically as they waited. It was slightly after seven. The announcement was supposed to come between seven and eight.

We finished eating and waited another fifteen minutes on the edges of our seats. Something started happening on-screen. I heard the voices of the commentator and his assistant.

"It sounds as if…as if…the winner has been chosen!"

Amid a buzz of excitement, a man in a suit walked to the white-board. He taped a piece of paper next to the one reading *Akutagawa Prize*.

Keiko Nishikawa
Dregs

Suddenly, the reporters were in a flurry. The commentator let out an excited cry. An announcement played over the loudspeakers.

"This year's Akutagawa Prize is awarded to *Dregs* by Keiko Nishikawa. Copies of the winning book will be placed on the table at the front of the room. A press conference with Keiko Nishikawa…"
I wondered how many people were watching the broadcast at that moment. Watching at home, on the train, in pubs and offices. The news would spread on social media, and tomorrow it would be the top news in papers and TV shows.

How was my sister feeling at that moment? What was my dad doing?

As I watched the screen in a daze, Hino said, "She won… She did it! Your sister is amazing. She won the Akutagawa Prize!"

Our eyes met. It didn't feel real.

"Thanks. I'm really happy for her."

That was all I said. Then Wataya smiled wryly.

"I thought she'd win. She'll be the darling of the media. Are you gonna start walking around with your nose in the air, Little Brother?"

I thought about that. *Nose… Pinocchio… Rudolph…*

"Damn it, I can't think of a good joke!" I moaned. The two of them laughed.

The Naoki Prize winner was announced next. My sister's press conference happened first. Cameras flashed, and she was bombarded with questions from reporters. She answered concisely. The press conference only lasted about ten minutes. I felt a little distracted. My heart was still pounding. But I knew I couldn't stay in Hino's house. I told her and Wataya that I needed to head home. While Wataya distracted Hino's parents, we whispered goodbye outside the front door.

"See you tomorrow. Good night."

"Good night. Thank you for today."

The Hino who would only exist for this one day parted ways with the me who would go on to tomorrow.

As I stepped onto the sidewalk, I looked back and thought I saw the curtain in the living room window flutter. Was it Hino's father? The figure looked like a man, but I wasn't sure. He might have seen me…

I walked to my bike. As I stood next to it absently, lit up by the streetlight, I sensed someone approaching. I turned around. It was Wataya, pushing her bike.

"There you go spacing out again. Maori's mom kept saying she'd take me home. It was awful. But I told her I'd ride my bike, so could you come along with me? Actually, you're so out of it; I should be the one taking you home!"

That would definitely not be right, so I told her I'd ride back with her to her house. We talked on the way to her apartment. I don't exactly remember what we discussed, but I have a sense that she chose a cheerful topic for my sake. When we got to her building, I headed home alone, despite her worries.

On the ride back to my apartment complex, all I could think about was my sister. It was after nine when I got back. Dad was sitting in the kitchen waiting for me. He had a somber expression on his face. The laptop was next to him, along with a can of low-malt beer.

I had a bad feeling about this. He looked up at me.

"Tooru, is Keiko Nishikawa…"

I looked at him, forgetting to blink.

"Sanae?"

4

I didn't say anything, so Dad continued.

"Today, they announced the Akutagawa Prize. I wanted to know who won, so just now I looked online and saw that Keiko Nishikawa did. A young woman in her twenties. I knew the name. And when I saw the picture from the press conference, I knew it was Sanae. Did you know? Tooru…did you know?"

I'd predicted this day would come eventually. Even as I rode home from Hino's house, it had been in the back of my mind. I'd also figured that when that time did come, Dad and I would have a serious talk.

"I knew," I said. "We kept it secret from you, but Sanae started writing novels a long time ago. Under the pen name Keiko Nishikawa."

"You're kidding me. And she moved out to become a novelist? She was escaping from us?"

"She wasn't escaping. She was heading toward something."

"It's the same thing."

"No, it's completely different. She didn't run from her own life. She ran toward it."

Dad cast his eyes down, frowning. He sighed, and then, after a pause, he said, "Did you meet with her?"

It felt like I was watching a bad movie. Only the ticking of the clock marked reality passing by.

"We weren't in regular contact, but recently, she had a signing event at a bookstore. We met there by chance and talked."

"Is she coming back?"

"She has her own life now."

"What, she doesn't want to live with us anymore?"

Dad looked up and, without meeting my eyes, looked down again.

"It's not that, but she worked hard for our sake for a long time. Starting from her first year in junior high, she kept our family together. You have to let her walk her own path now."

I said that, but I too had been waiting for her to come back. Until I met Hino and Wataya and created my own world, that had been my only wish. I had even believed that was my life.

"What will happen to us?" Dad asked.

"We'll keep doing what we've been doing. I'm already studying for the civil service exam. The two of us can make it work."

"She's making a fool of me."

"Why do you think that?"

"I'm no good as a father, no good as a novelist—No, I'm not even a novelist. She looks down on me for it."

"That's not true."

"Then why did she move out without saying anything?"

I stared at Dad in the silent room. He must have felt my gaze, but he kept averting his eyes.

"If she told you, you would've tried to stop her, wouldn't you? And then she wouldn't have been able to go. So…"

"So what? It's not fair to leave without telling anyone. We're a family."

A family. When my sister and I had needed a father, Dad wasn't there for us. That was the one thing I couldn't let myself say. I relaxed the fist I had been clenching.

"That's right. We're a family. So let's celebrate her win."

"Ever since I was a boy, I dreamed of winning the Akutagawa Prize. I got pretty close to getting the New Author Prize, you know."

"She won because she's your daughter. She grew up surrounded by the books you bought."

"Ah, so that's how you try to boost my ego and smooth this over? Even you have a girlfriend. If you get married, you'll probably move out. I'll be left alone."

I thought of Hino's smile with a twinge of pain. I had no idea where our relationship would go. Or what would happen with her amnesia.

"Get married? I can't even imagine that right now."

"Is that so?… I guess I'm pretty drunk."

"You are. And I'm going to tell you something: You're drunk on yourself, too. On your being a widower. On yourself as the struggling author. On the delusion that maybe you can become a novelist."

Normally, I wouldn't speak that harshly to him, but for the first time in ages, he met my eyes. He might turn his face toward me as he spoke or joked around with me, but he never actually stared straight at me. He had always avoided it, just like he evaded facing the truth.

But he wasn't the only one. I'd avoided it, too.

I'd been running away this whole time. Everything stayed the same, and I didn't try to change it.

Awkwardness filled the room. I sat there silently. Our eyes shifted away from each other.

"What the hell are you talking about?"

Dad stood up, his can of beer in one hand, and started walking toward his room. As I watched him go, I thought about some things.

Would today be another day where I didn't try to change anything? Would I keep running away tomorrow and the next day, pretending nothing had happened? Would I leave the discord in our family as it was, without saying what I really wanted to say?

What should I do? Couldn't anyone tell me? Anyone?

Suddenly, I thought of Hino. It didn't happen very often, but occasionally, there was a little friction or misunderstanding between us, like with the straw hat. I tried to pretend I didn't notice it, didn't see it. After all, it was insignificant compared to the big problems she was dealing with. I saw her living the best life she could every day. Time, possibilities, even her future had been stolen from her. Nevertheless, she tried to stay optimistic.

What had I seen in her room earlier? What had I stolen a glance at? She faced hardship every day. What about me? Was I going to run away at the very moment I had a chance to change things? Was I okay with that? I had no idea what would happen with me and Hino. But I wanted to be a person she could feel proud of. Before I knew it, I was following Dad and grabbing his shoulder.

"Dad. We have to change. We can't run away anymore."

I guess I caught him off guard, because he shook my hand off and turned toward me.

"I'm not running away. I just don't have talent. If I had talent, I could become a novelist tomorrow. I could rebuild my life plan."

He was glaring at me. I was taller than him now.

"So let yourself get hurt. Fail a few times. And learn something from it."

"What are you talking about? I've been hurt plenty."

"Get over yourself. I guess it's easier that way, isn't it? Making yourself the hero of a tragedy. Write a novel about it, say it's your entry in the New Author contest you never enter."

My words drained all trace of emotion from my father's face.

I knew the truth. He was trying to be a novelist, but at the same time, he'd already given up.

"I'm—I'm not doing that."

"Don't lie to me."

"It's the truth. I genuinely want to be a writer. Even now, that's my plan in life."

"Dad, I'm tired of lies. You don't submit it because you don't want to be hurt. Isn't that right? You wanted to be a novelist, didn't you? Then—then stop being afraid of getting hurt!"

"Tooru!"

He grabbed my collar. We stared at each other at close range. Would today be the day he raised a hand at me for the first time?

I didn't care if he did. If you want to move forward in life, you have to experience pain. You can't run from it. You can't get drunk on yourself and evade it.

We didn't look away from each other this time. I steeled myself for whatever was coming. But it wasn't anger in his eyes; it was misery…

"So, you knew. You knew I wasn't submitting my stories. That I wasn't sending in the manuscripts."

Suddenly my breath grew ragged. Or maybe it had been all along, and I'd just noticed it. Dad lowered his hand from my collar.

"I'm sorry. Once when I was cleaning your room, I saw all the envelopes in your closet. Envelopes you'd addressed and stuffed with your manuscripts but never sent. It wasn't proof, but it was enough to make me wonder. Maybe you weren't entering the contest anymore. Maybe you'd given up."

Instead of looking at me, Dad stared down at the dull flooring.

"But, Dad, there's something I want you to know. Sanae and I are grateful to you. You work from morning to night to support us. You're supporting me right now. You might not be a novelist, but you're a good father. The only thing is, we have to stop running from the truth."

That was everything I wanted to say to him. All that was left was to wait for his reaction. Time passed so slowly, I felt like I was watching a sandglass. I don't know how long we stood there in silence.

"We've never talked like this, have we?" he mumbled. I looked at him. He was desperately trying to smile.

"No, we haven't," I muttered.

"You've changed lately. I think it started around the time you started dating your girlfriend."

"Yeah…you could be right. She's a fantastic person."

"Is she? I'm glad you met a good one. Just treat her well, okay?"

I nodded. Dad took a deep breath and let it out.

"So I shouldn't be afraid of getting hurt, is that it? Yes, you're right."

He sounded like he was finally sobering up after a long bender.

"I'm sorry if I said too much," I said.

"No…I'm the one who needs to apologize. I'm sorry. I've been running away for a long time… Running from reality. I ran from the housework, letting Sanae and you do it all. And to top it all off, I quit submitting to the contest. Like you said, I was afraid of getting hurt. After losing your mom, I was afraid of learning I didn't have what it takes to write. So I ran away."

Maybe his strength had run out, because he sat down limply where he was. I hesitated, then decided to sit next to him. We didn't know what to do next. Dad looked down at his half-empty beer can and squeezed the sides in.

If we were characters in a book, I wonder how we would have understood each other. Life didn't play out like fiction. Reality was drier, with the characters at a loss for what to do. We sat there like we'd sunk into the floor.

But the world keeps moving. I asked Dad if he wanted me to cook something. He said not to worry about it.

If I knew one thing for sure, it was that we conveyed to each other our important feelings. That counted as a step forward. From now on, no matter what happened, I wouldn't run away. I would keep looking Dad in the eye. I'm sure he was lost in thought at that moment, too.

After a while of sitting in silence, Dad said, "Actually, would you mind making something?"

I looked up. He made a poor attempt at a smile.

"For some reason, I'm in the mood for tattered eggs."

It was one of his favorite dishes, one Sanae used to make a lot. Mom's family used to make it, I guess.

I put half a block of tofu in a small pot and added stock powder, soy sauce, mirin, and sugar. Then I stirred in some beaten eggs and cooked until the liquid was reduced. I don't know the real name of the dish, but we call it tattered eggs.

When it was done, Dad put a big serving of rice in a bowl. He looked at me with an embarrassed expression, but also like he wanted something. That was his way of communicating.

Lazy bum, I thought and spooned the tattered eggs over his rice. My sister said it was poor manners to eat them like that, but he'd always liked them that way and done it behind her back. As he sat in the kitchen chair wolfing down the rice and eggs, he said, "Hey…next time, would you show me how to make these?"

I stared at him. He smiled guiltily.

"I'm sorry. I can't change all at once. But, you know, I've been looking for the chance. And…"

He tried hard to hold his smile.

That's true of everyone, I think. We all want to be good people. Dad and I had been avoiding the truth, but that didn't make us bad people. We'd just lost sight of the light. I knew that now, because Hino had given it back to me. I couldn't help grinning at Dad's uncomfortable smile, which he also returned.

The two of us cleaned up the dishes. It was almost ten. The landline, which almost no one ever calls, started ringing. Dad looked puzzled for a second but then seemed to realize something and looked at me. I nodded at him. He picked up the receiver, looking nervous.

"Hello… Oh, Sanae?"

He looked at me again. I pretended not to notice. I walked over to the window and opened it. A fresh night breeze blew into the house. Behind me, my father and sister were talking for the first time in years.

"No, not at all. I'm the one who needs to apologize. I've been a bad father. And I… No, I won't say any more. I'm sorry. But, Sanae, isn't today a special day for you? Yes. Yes, I was surprised. I couldn't believe it was my own daughter. Yes."

After a while, he sniffled and said very emotionally, "Sanae, congratulations. From the bottom of my heart, congratulations."

I felt the core of my being tremble. I looked silently up at the sky.

I cried just a little.

About ten days after the announcement of the prize, my sister visited home.

"You've kept things looking very nice, as expected of my little brother," she said when she came in.

She'd called a second time a few days earlier, and ever since, Dad had been in high spirits. Starting the morning after our talk, he'd been helping with the chores. He tried cooking some stuff, messed it up, and tried again with my help, learning little by little. The day of her visit, he'd been cleaning since morning, and he boasted that he was going to cook dinner.

"I'm not the only one cleaning," I told Sanae. "Dad's been helping."

She looked genuinely surprised.

"I've turned over a new leaf," Dad said bashfully. "Cooking and cleaning are kind of fun once you give them a try. I'm going to take a break from writing for a while. It's not an escape. It's just that I want to wait until I can really face myself in my writing. Then I'll start up again. By the way, Sanae, feel free to take any books you want. That includes first editions. I need to pare down my collection."

Sanae gazed at him. He looked at the ground, then smiled shyly.

"You…you were the reason I started writing in the first place," she said. "Thanks to you, I was able to watch someone writing novels up close. At first, I was like you. I wrote to escape from my reality. Then after a while, I stopped doing that. I started to think that maybe writing was a way for me to grow, a way for me to encounter my own new words and my own new ideas."

Dad was silent. He looked moved almost to the point of tears. My sister was watching him, but then she took a cheerful tone, clearly trying to brighten the mood.

"And…yes, you're right. This house does have a few too many books. It's not very sanitary. I think I'll take you up on your offer to bring some home with me. Is that all right, Dad?"

"Yes, of course. Go ahead. It's for the best."

"Are you sure? I'm going to be merciless."

The two of them grinned at the same moment.

I wouldn't say that all the bad blood disappeared right then and there. Dad had chosen being a novelist over being a father. My sister took over the household for him even though she knew his dream wasn't coming true but eventually chose the writer's path herself. Both felt guilty for their actions.

All the same, they both smiled. Each in their own way, they were trying to move forward.

Our air conditioner doesn't work very well, so it was hot in our house, but it was a nice summer day. The kind of day where you can almost feel the sunrays brushing against your skin.

5

August 26 (Tuesday), Summer Vacation

Morning at home: as usual.

Afternoon at home: Sketching. Did seven drawings based on scenes from foreign films. Going shockingly well. While drawing, I feel surprised by how accurate my lines are. Afterward, can't help smiling at my pieces. Got carried away and did five more drawings until hand started to ache. Gave myself a massage so as not to be a burden on tomorrow's me.

With my boyfriend: Talked with him today at the library about fireworks. On the last day of summer vacation, there's going to be a fireworks show in the neighboring district.

I waffled but ultimately decided to invite him. He agreed right away. Yesss!

I've never been to that show before, but my boyfriend said he's been with his sister and dad in elementary school. He said his sister is staying with them for the first time in years.

Interesting. I suggested he invite her, too, but he got flustered. He tries to act cool, so it's cute when he gets like that.

He said he'll ask his sister about the fireworks, and afterward, we went to the bookstore. There are some books I read before my accident that I wanted to try reading again. I also want to rent movies my past selves haven't seen and find some new favorites. Novels are harder because they take so long to read, but movies and manga are doable. I bought a bunch of manga with interesting titles.

My boyfriend spent the time reading a magazine that had an interview with his sister in it. I went up and whispered that he had a thing for his sister, and he got all flustered and muttered something.

When it was time to go home, he asked if I'd forgotten my straw hat again. I guess I made a mistake before. I forgot we'd looked at straw hats together. I'd written down that he wanted to buy one for me as a present, but I didn't check my notes. Then I went and bought it myself.

I brushed it off by saying the size wasn't quite right. He took something out of his bag. It was a hat decoration. A fake sunflower with a pin on the back. He said he thought it would look good on the straw hat and gave it to me shyly. I think he realized that my past selves hadn't been wearing it because we didn't want him to feel bad.

How can he be so kind?

I thought about today, just like my other selves did before. Even when I forget important things, he doesn't mind and is still kind to me, like today.

I held the sunflower tight as I watched him ride away on his bike. My heart was throbbing like it was trying to tell me something.

I think I might be falling for him.

I haven't been able to calm down since I read my journal this morning.

Today is August 31. The last day of summer vacation. I checked my planner, and it is definitely the day we planned to go see the fireworks together.

When I woke up, I saw a yukata folded on my desk. Yesterday's me must have gotten it ready. There was a Post-it note on top with a drawing of myself saying *Have enough fun for the both of us! Love, Yesterday's You.*

I look out the window. The world is brimming with the pure white light of a summer afternoon. The scene is like the canvas of a fickle painter. Yesterday, it was full of new leaves, but today it's covered over with new paint. The landscape has been redrawn.

I calm my nerves and check my plans again. The fireworks begin at seven. I'm supposed to meet my boyfriend outside the station in the neighboring district at four. We're hoping to avoid the crowds and have a chance to take our time talking with each other.

Izumi isn't coming. I invited her, but she told me to go have fun with my boyfriend since it would be the last big event of the summer.

Time flies as I read my binder and journal. At two, I put on the yukata. A past me has already found a video that shows how to wear and tie the cotton kimono, and by watching that, I'm able to do it by myself with no problem.

The white kimono had a subdued pattern with blue flowers. Apparently, I borrowed it from Mom, which explains why it looks kind of adult.

I stand in front of the mirror and put my hair in an updo. A little makeup finishes off the look. Actually, not quite. Along with the yukata, a fake sunflower is set out on my desk with a note on it.

It might be nice to wear the sunflower. Your boyfriend gave it to you, it reads.

This morning when I woke up, I had amnesia. When I read the binder and journal to cheer myself up, I found out I had a boyfriend. This unknown boyfriend of mine had given me a present.

I'd expect to feel confused. My former self sure would have. But…

I pick up the fake sunflower. It seems I usually pin it to my straw hat, but it wouldn't be half bad in my hair. I gently attach it with a hairpin. It's not my usual style, but oddly enough, I kind of like it. Part of me seems to feel the fake sunflower is special.

I think I might be falling for him.

That line from my diary flickers across my mind, but I push it aside.

I've already prepared everything I need to bring, so I decide to head out, even though it's a little early. Since riding a bike in a yukata would be dangerous, Mom agrees to take me to the station. She offers to take me all the way to the neighboring district, where we've agreed to meet, but that would be embarrassing, so I turn down the offer.

At the station, I board a train and take it to the meeting spot. The station isn't very crowded yet. I'm ten minutes early, so I figure I'll go to the convenience store, but then someone comes up to me.

"Hino."

I turn around and see a skinny guy wearing a dark blue yukata. He smiles when he sees my face. It's my boyfriend, same as the photo I looked at before I left home.

What's going on? My heart is beating faster than usual.

"Oh, um, h-hi."

I'm confused because I wasn't expecting him to be there yet. Maybe he notices, because he looks sad for a second. Damn it. From his perspective, all he did was say hi to his girlfriend, so why would she be confused?

"Your yukata looks really good on you," he says.

"What, really? Thanks. Yours looks good, too. I'm impressed. Did you put it on yourself?"

"Yeah. But guys' yukata are easy. I practiced this morning."

"Wow…you practiced wearing it? Wait, were you naked underneath?"

"Honestly, is that all you think about?"

I manage to break through the awkwardness with a joke.

No matter how close we get, or how well we understand each other, I'll forget it all. He doesn't know that. Or does he?

"Want to go to a café or something while we wait? If you don't mind going to a regular coffee shop, I'll pick up the tab," he offers kindly, interrupting my thoughts.

"That's not like my boyfriend! Nice try, but today we're splitting the tab."

"Then I'll keep my extra cash for the fireworks," he says as we head toward the café.

There are several other couples wearing yukata in the café next to the station. A waiter brings us to a table by the window, and we sit down.

"So, your sister is coming today, right?" I say. Supposedly, I suggested that she come with us a couple of days ago. I guess I thought it would be nice since she's back home. When he brought it up with her, she'd said she'd like to meet for a little while at the festival.

"Yeah. We're supposed to meet her at six at the bridge near the venue."

"Oh, okay. I'm a little nervous."

I think I really do feel anxious. I'm being more polite than usual, too.

"Interesting. I didn't know you could get nervous."

"Of course I do. Like when… Hmm, I can't think of anything."

As I rack my brain, my boyfriend smiles. I pout, and he apologizes.

"Don't feel so intimidated by my sister. We're just saying hi, so you don't need to worry."

"I know I was the one who suggested it, but she's a celebrity now, right? Can she walk around in public like this?"

"She says people don't recognize her as often as you'd think. There will be lots of people here, and she said she'd be fine if she wears her hair differently."

After that, we talk until after five thirty. There are more people wearing yukata now, and some of them start getting ready to leave. We do the same.

A few minutes' walk from the café, the fireworks show will be held along the river that runs through downtown. Local restaurants and bars have set up booths outside, and there are stalls like you'd see at a festival. The street is already crowded.

As you'd expect at a fireworks show, there are lots of couples. Some are holding hands. My boyfriend seems to notice, but he doesn't say anything. What should I do? Should I just do it? I've never held hands with a boy before, but I wouldn't mind. I glance at his manly hand, the tendons clearly visible.

Here goes!

Before I know it, I'm reaching out for his hand. He shoots me a surprised look. I pretend to be calm and meet his gaze. But my heart is pounding in my ears.

"Wh-what are you doing, Hino?"

"Nothing, I just thought this way, we wouldn't get separated. Also, since we're meeting your sister, I thought we could try acting like a couple."

"You're pretty daring."

"You noticed?" I say.

I'm talking faster than usual. I feel embarrassed to be acting like this, but today's me will only exist for today. I don't want to have any regrets about this day.

We walk along, holding hands, not like a fake couple. Like a real couple.

As we get closer to the venue, the crowd becomes so dense, we can hardly move.

It feels even more real now. I suddenly have a boyfriend, and we're together at the last fireworks show of the summer.

"I can't believe I'm doing this. I'm at a fireworks show with my boyfriend," I murmur.

"Where did that come from?" he asks.

"I don't know. It didn't feel real, like my feet weren't on the ground… but suddenly I realized it is real, and I guess it made me happy," I say to cover up the real reason.

He gives me a fresh-faced smile.

"Let's have fun, Hino. I'm kind of weak and incompetent, but I can beat anyone when it comes to sincerity."

Weak and incompetent but sincere? I can't help smiling at that self-description.

"I've never heard a speech that's so pitiful and so hopeful at the same time."

His grin widens. I squeeze his hand.

As the crimson sky slowly fades, the festival begins to light up with brilliant colors, as if to decorate the end of summer. I don't even mind the muggy weather. As we head toward the bridge where we'll meet his sister, a cool breeze starts to blow.

"Ah, that feels good," I utter. He looks at me with gentle eyes.

"Tooru! I'm glad I was able to find you so easily," a thin, clear voice calls out.

I face toward it and see an amazing beauty. It's my boyfriend's sister. I've seen pictures of her online, but her skin glows differently in real life.

"Hi, Sanae. Hey, what's this about?" my boyfriend says, noticing something.

I follow his gaze and see a man wearing a white polo shirt who's probably in his fifties. They do look alike…

"You came, too, Dad?"

"Uh, I'm the escort. Sanae's. She's famous, after all."

So it *is* their dad. I definitely did not expect him to be here. I'm instantly nervous.

He notices me and, for some reason, looks momentarily frightened.

"…H-hello," I say awkwardly.

"N-nice to meet you," he responds.

Suddenly, he starts peering around and taps his chest pocket.

"I'm out of cigarettes; I'll go buy some," he says and disappears into the crowd.

My boyfriend's sister, who's wearing an elegant indigo yukata, turns to him with a troubled smile.

"I'm sorry. I was planning to come alone, but when I mentioned your girlfriend, Dad suddenly said he wanted to come along. And he doesn't even smoke!"

My boyfriend smiles amusingly.

"It's fine. I'm just surprised. Maybe, in his own way, he's trying to face reality head-on. He even shaved properly. Or maybe he just didn't want to be left alone at home."

Trying to face reality?

That confuses me, but my boyfriend and his sister both seem to understand. They're smiling, and somehow, they look like they're thinking of someone they love very much.

Finally, his sister looks at me. Her gaze falls on our hands, which are still joined. She smiles.

"Pleased to meet you. You're Tooru's girlfriend, I believe?"

"Yes, yes, I am! Pleased to meet you. Thank you for inviting me…oh, no, you didn't. Um, I'm dating Tooru. My name is Maori Hino."

This might just be a quick hello, but I still feel nervous. I garble my self-introduction, but I manage better than with the dad. I bow my head, and she bows back.

"I'm Sanae Kamiya, Tooru's sister. It's a pleasure to meet you."

I look at her face again. At first, I didn't think they looked alike, but now I can see the resemblance. Their kind eyes are identical. As I fall deep into them, she smiles again.

"Well, we've met now, so why don't you two go enjoy the festival? I'm going to look for our father."

"What, already?" I say, trying to keep her with us. She makes a face that I would describe as elegantly mischievous.

"Thank you for your kindness, but I don't want to interrupt your date… Isn't that right, Tooru?" she says.

"You're not interrupting anything," he replies in a flurry.

She looks at him like she finds his reaction adorable.

"Take care, you two. Maori, I look forward to meeting again," she says and slips into the crowd in the same direction as her father. A relieved sigh escapes my lips.

"Wow, I was so nervous. Your sister is so beautiful in real life!" I exclaim.

"That's my sister for you. She's finally able to do what she wants, and it's taken the edge off a little," he answers, looking proudly into the distance.

"Huh. Oh, by the way, did something happen with your dad? I was interested in what you two were saying about him," I say. My boyfriend shifts his gaze, then stares straight at me.

"To tell the truth, I wasn't getting along with him so well. But recently we had a good talk about it."

He tells me about his family situation, the conflict with his dad, and the reconciliation with Sanae. When he's done, I look down.

"Wow, I had no idea all that happened after you left my house that night," I say.

He builds his life up like that, day by day. The progress is gradual, but he's moving forward. What about me? I can feel him watching me as I think about these things.

"But you know what, Hino? The reason I was able to have that talk with him was because of you."

"What? I didn't do anything, though!"

I stare at him, puzzled, but he just smiles silently.

He probably said it to be nice, but that doesn't really fit with his personality. Did I actually do something? I feel like I'm always receiving more than giving. Did I manage to give something back? If I did…it feels like salvation.

Without meaning to, I squeeze his hand. He squeezes back.

"Let's go. This festival will only last for tonight. Let's enjoy it."

"Yeah! Let's go!"

We blend in with the festival crowds. We play around like all the other couples, get all the food we can carry, buy things we don't need, and have a ball doing stuff we don't normally do.

We buy *takoyaki*. I eat one, and it's really good, so I stab another with a toothpick and hold it out for my boyfriend. He turns his face away, embarrassed. It's funny, so I tease him. "At least use a different toothpick," he mumbles.

Oops…would that be like an indirect kiss? Now I feel embarrassed.

We go to the shooting range. I go for the big prizes without much luck. His arms and legs are longer, and he wins a steady stream of smaller stuff.

I tell him he should dream big since he's a guy. He answers that small pleasures are important. On my next shot, I hit a card that says *Free Gift*, and it falls to the ground. We're both super excited. Except, it turns out to be a bunch of candy, which is basically the same prizes my boyfriend got. It's still fun, though.

I laugh a lot. We fit enough memories for a whole summer into one day.

I have a really good time, feeling as if I've never had more fun in my entire life. I feel naturally attracted to him, and toward me, he is affectionate.

Finally, it's time for the fireworks. We sit on the riverbank together and watch them. I used to always be uncomfortable in big crowds. But tonight I feel soothed knowing we're just two insignificant people among all the others.

Just like everyone else, we look up at the fireworks, grow speechless with awe, and hold each other's hand tightly.

Suddenly, I think about the fate of my feelings.

Will the emotions I feel today vanish by tomorrow, just like my memories? They won't take root, will they? Does my mind treat them like information so that it's impossible for them to accumulate over time?

I hope something can remain. I hope the feeling I have right now carries over to the me of tomorrow. I hope I don't forget.

"I…don't want to forget," I say before thinking. Tears blur my vision.

Why? What's going on? The tears won't stop.

Of course I don't want to forget! I don't want to forget such an important moment and for it to only exist within my diary. I mean, you only live once. You can't get back a moment in time. That's why people cherish their memories.

It's too awful to think that I won't be able to remember this. It's too sad.

My boyfriend watches me wipe away my tears with the hand that's not holding his.

"I won't forget this day," he says. I can hear his voice clearly through the rumbling of the fireworks.

"I—I won't, either. How could I forget… It's so strange. I must have had too much fun. I can't stop crying."

As I cry softly, he squeezes my hand tight.

"It's human nature to forget. But don't worry. No memory disappears completely. I believe that," he says.

I look at this kind human as I desperately try to stop crying.

Once again, I wonder if maybe he knows about my amnesia. If possibly he knows, he notices it, but he pretends he doesn't? If…if that's true…then maybe I don't have anything to fear.

I squeeze his hand back and make a wish. *Please. I'll be as kind as I can. I won't be selfish. I'll be grateful for my parents every day. Please just let me stay with him. Somehow, somehow.*

For a second, probably because of my tears, he seems to disappear before my eyes. In a panic, I tighten my grip. He grips back.

"Tooru, please don't go anywhere."

"Don't worry. I'll always be by your side."

Another unattainable dreamlike flower blossoms in the night sky, drowning out his voice.

The Blankness of Blanks

1

Summer vacation is over, and the fall semester is starting. Which means three months have passed since Maori and Kamiya started dating.

I'll never forget that day at the end of May. After school, this guy who Maori didn't even know stopped her in the hall out of the blue. Later, when we met up in front of the library, she told me she decided to go out with him. I was shocked to my core.

Maori has a problem with her memory. She can't keep new memories for more than a day. If she meets a stranger, the next morning, they're back to being a stranger again. I couldn't believe she was trying to have a boyfriend under those conditions.

"But why?" I asked.

"He told me he likes me. So I thought I'd try dating him."

"I don't get it. You said his name's Kamiya? Did you tell this guy about your amnesia?"

"Nope, and I don't plan to. But I thought that maybe, even now, I could do something new, and that made me want to try."

The next day during break, I went to talk to the guy. He didn't have a single distinguishing feature. When I asked him about Maori, he didn't have much to say. I figured they'd break up quickly. Even though he told her he liked her, he didn't seem like he did.

Though, as it turned out, they've been dating way longer than I ever imagined.

At some point, Kamiya changed. The first time I noticed was when I watched them riding a bike together. Even as a bystander, I could tell how much he cared about Maori. Now that I think about it, he probably knew about her amnesia by then. But why did he suddenly change? Wouldn't most people break up if they learned their partner had amnesia?

Fall semester started, and the first few days flew past. One afternoon, I'm walking behind the two of them on the way to the station, watching them side by side, when suddenly, Kamiya turns around.

"What, do I have something stuck to me?" he asks, playing dumb.

"Your head," I respond, just to say something.

"If that wasn't stuck to me, I'd be in trouble," he answers.

"Don't worry, boyfriend," Maori says. "If it falls off, I'll find a nice new one for you."

"Hino, I'm not some character from *Anpanman*."

Maori's amnesia—it's called anterograde amnesia—isn't something that's easy to fix. To start with, there's no treatment. It might be cured all of a sudden next week, or a year might pass without anything changing. Or three years or five. Both Maori and her family, and the other people who support her, will need to persevere.

Yet…I think Kamiya might be able to support her more than her family or I can.

Helping her get through her daily life has already changed him. She told me she saw him almost every day over summer break. He was also the one who encouraged her to start drawing again. It turns out, even though her brain can't retain memories, muscle memory can persist over time. Embarrassingly enough, that never occurred to me.

Ever since Maori started drawing, she's been more emotionally stable. I haven't told Kamiya this, but she had a major breakdown before. Her parents and I had been afraid that would happen. One day in the middle of May, without any warning, she stayed home from school. She didn't answer when I texted or called. I was worried and stopped by her house after school. When I arrived, her mother's face stiffened.

Although her memories are reset every day, her emotions aren't. Due to chemicals in the brain and other factors, the emotional state from the day before can carry over sometimes. That morning, when Maori woke up and her mom explained that she had amnesia, she said she couldn't bear it.

"There's no point in living like that," her mom told me she shouted. "Just leave me alone."

She stayed in her room all day and wouldn't eat.

Maori's mom often worried about a certain possibility. Maori's doctor had told her that in some cases, depression can be a complication of anterograde amnesia. It makes sense. If I was in Maori's situation, I probably wouldn't even be able to go to school. I'd be so pessimistic about the future that the situation might spiral into something even worse.

I got permission from Maori's mom to go stand outside her door. When I said hi, she told me she didn't want to see me. "I'm sorry I've caused you so much trouble," she said. "But today, I just can't handle it."

I was forced to acknowledge my own powerlessness. I thought of trying to talk to her, but there was nothing I could say that would comfort her. If only my weirdness could have made her laugh at that moment. But I couldn't think of the right thing to say.

"Okay, well, I guess I'll go home, then," I said.

The next day, from the moment she woke up, she was in low spirits. When I asked why, she said that yesterday's Maori had written about what happened the day before in her journal. She apologized for pushing me away when I'd gone to the trouble of coming to see her. The best I could do was play dumb and tell her with a smile to cheer up. After school, we ate a lot of sweets together.

I should have told her the day before to not write anything down in her journal. However, I hadn't felt comfortable saying that. Instead, I told her a day late as we demolished a piece of cake. She looked like she was going to cry.

"That makes sense. I'll get rid of yesterday's entry," she said sadly.

I wasn't able to leave an impact or fill her journal with happy memories. But Kamiya managed to do it. I don't attribute it simply to the power of love. Still, at this very moment, Maori is smiling.

"Oh, I almost forgot. I want to draw you again, Tooru. I improved a lot over vacation, you know," she says.

"Sure, but even if you're a better artist, that doesn't make my face any more handsome," he answers.

"In that case, I'll draw some roses or something in the background. Ba-ding!"

"Behind my wry smile? That will be one surreal drawing."

Even though Maori can't store new memories, I've noticed that she takes less time to become comfortable around Kamiya now and smiles at him more. Will they go on like this? I haven't told anyone, but sometimes I feel a little jealous of them.

They continue, their relationship remaining unchanged right through Sports Day and the school festival. Fall comes, and cold winds blow. They're still dating.

I observe them as the seasons change. In fall, Maori's mental state becomes unstable again. She comes to school every day, but she seems upset right from the morning. It makes sense. In her mind, yesterday was April, but when she wakes up, almost half a year has gone by. Then, when she gets to school, she's forced to think about her career options. Even worse, she's probably comparing herself to me.

Even if she graduates from high school, she won't be able to go to college. There's a limit to what you can do with the knowledge of a second-year high school student. She'd have a difficult time at a technical college, too, and getting a job wouldn't be easy.

She doesn't let on what a hard worker she is, but I know. She must feel so frustrated. Every day, she has to face the reality of everything she'd created falling apart. She's been left behind by time, by the future.

But she has Kamiya.

After school, he's there with her, trying to make her day enjoyable. When she's with him, she smiles like she's forgotten all about her morning depression. Even when he's not there, she gradually becomes more cheerful as the day goes on. I start to be overwhelmed by schoolwork and studying for tests, and I have less time to spend with her. The days fly by.

It's the winter of our second year in high school now. Around Christmas, Maori starts knitting. Each day's self makes a little more progress on the scarf she's making for Kamiya. Kamiya bakes a cake to surprise her.

On New Year's Day, the three of us make our first shrine visit of the year in the evening. When the first snow of the year falls, Kamiya and Maori pile it up to make a snowman after school.

When she's with him, she laughs. He makes her smile.

Sometimes I feel like asking him how he has the energy to do it. If I did, I'm sure he'd just say, "Because I love her." Even if he sounds nonchalant, I think he probably cares about her even more than I do.

One day in the middle of February after the three of us hung out and Maori has gone home, I ask him that question. Without cracking a smile, he says exactly what I expected.

I'm forced to think about the meaning of love. In the past, I saw two people who loved each other deeply begin to hate each other because of trivial things. They argued about all kinds of things, like the way their schedules didn't match or how they viewed money differently. Though, that wasn't really what happened. They simply both fell in love with other people. They steadily grew apart. One of them worried about their reputation, so instead of divorcing, they decided to live separately.

I'm talking about my parents, of course.

I don't think that's the only reason, but for a while, I stopped trusting people. I didn't tell anyone, though. I can't go to anyone for advice. I have to heal my own wounds. I'm a solitary animal.

By junior high, people were saying I was cold, and they didn't know what I was thinking. They were partly right. Not many people approached me, but when I entered high school, Maori talked to me like it was completely natural. I thought she seemed like an interesting person.

We kept talking, and pretty soon, we were best friends. I'd regained my faith in humankind.

"Because I love her."

Kamiya says those words casually. But I think he cares about Maori even more than I do.

Love is an emotion, a feeling. It's not an act of will or logic. If you fall in love with someone, you might be able to think of a reason afterward, but that reason is distinct from the actual sensation of loving them.

People don't fall in love for a specific reason. Love truly is rooted in feelings with no logic supporting it.

"Just because you love someone, does that mean you'll do anything for them? Personally, I don't get that," I say self-mockingly.

He thinks for a minute before answering. "I don't do anything. I do what I can."

"Is that true? You seem to be pushing yourself kind of hard for someone who's just doing what they can," I say, grilling him a little. He stares at the twilight sky.

"I don't do what's impossible, and I couldn't even if I tried. But if there's something I can do with a little extra effort or something I want to do, then I feel happy to do it."

I don't think I'll ever forget the look on his face at that moment. Somehow, that kind, average face of his seems to glow.

"My life before I met her was boring. I thought I knew all about life, and I never did anything stupid or crazy. I was like that since I was a kid. The truth is, I probably didn't believe in myself. I wasn't sickly or anything, but I did have a bunch of tests done at the doctor's, and I had a slight complex about being so skinny."

He's talking more passionately than he usually does. Suddenly, he smiles.

"But now I simply enjoy my days with Hino. I truly feel like if there's something I can do for her with a little extra effort, then I want to do it. She surprises me and makes me see things in a new light. She makes me feel like I want to be a better person."

He looks at me.

"You're probably going to laugh at me for saying embarrassing things again, right?" he says with a smile. I shake my head.

"It's interesting," I say, feeling like a lost child.

"But you help Hino out because you care about her, too, right?" he asks.

"I guess so. I think I'm a little more hands-off than you. Maori isn't quite normal right now, and I seek out things that aren't. It's interesting to me. Maybe that's why I stick with her. For my own selfish reasons," I say, but it's not quite true. I do care for her so, so much. Only, I'm powerless. I can't do anything for her…

"That might be partly true, but I don't think that's the whole story," Kamiya says.

"Is that so?"

"Yes. You know it, too, I think."

Winter is almost over when we have that conversation. Spring comes, bringing a breath of new life. Over spring break, the three of us hang out a few times. We have a picnic under the cherry blossom trees in a park that's famous for them.

"A poet once called cherry blossoms snow that never knew the sky," Kamiya says gracefully as I gaze up at the sky between the tree branches.

"I don't think I've heard that before. Snow that never knew the sky… It's true, the petals do look like snow," Maori says, sounding impressed. Kamiya looks at her with gentle eyes and smiles.

He tells us the story his sister told him about May sickness. He explains that after the busy spring ends, everyone gets lazy in May, and she called that "May sickness."

May… What will the three of us be doing this month?

I gaze up at the peach-colored snow that the sky never knew and think about that question. When our third year of high school starts, Maori and I will be in different classes. She won't be in the advanced class anymore. Before spring break started, the head teacher for our grade talked with Kamiya and arranged for Maori to be in his class.

In April, she and I start spending less time together at school. Before, Kamiya and Maori were only able to see each other after school. Now I watch them from the hallway talking to each other happily in class. At those times, I think about the meaning of love.

The procedural memory that Kamiya told me about is rooted in sensations. Does that mean that the sensation of love is carried from one day to the next inside Maori?

"I was so surprised. I'm a third-year student already, and I have a boyfriend, and he's in my class."

Even though I have a lot of studying to do, I still try to talk to Maori every night. I know now—she's made it through her second year, and she'll be okay from here on out. Kamiya is by her side. He knows about her amnesia, and he loves her anyway.

All the days blend together for me as I continue to study night and day. I've heard third year goes by quick because you're so focused on college entrance exams, and it's true.

Summer comes, a crucial time for test prep. By the time my pencil stops moving, it's fall. In winter, the Center Test looms near, and then after that, the second round of tests. Before I know it, it's spring. My long but short third year of high school is over.

We make it to high school graduation. All three of us.

Kamiya passed the civil service exam in the neighboring district, and this spring, he'll start working at city hall. Maori is making huge progress with drawing, and she'll be taking art class a few times a week while she waits for her amnesia to be cured. It's not that important, but I think I'll get into my first choice of university in our prefecture.

On the day of graduation, Maori says, "I can't believe it." The thing she can't believe isn't that so much time has passed. It's that she managed to stay in school long enough to graduate, even with her condition.

I really do think she'll be okay.

I watch her frolicking around with her diploma. Even though she has to face her situation all over again each time she wakes up in the morning, she'll be all right. She managed to stay in school and graduate. She has the journal that connects her past selves with her present self. She has her daily drawing practice and her ability to improve despite her memory loss. Even though she won't be able to see him every day anymore, she has Kamiya. If she has all of that, she'll be okay.

We spend the spring vacation after graduation getting ready for our next step in life. One day, the three of us go out like we used to.

"See you later! Thanks for today!"

Kamiya and I stand at the ticket gate, waving to Maori as she enters the station. The two of us have errands to run at the nearby mall, so Maori goes home first.

With no warning, Kamiya says, "Wataya…"

"What?"

He must have prepared himself mentally for this moment.

"There's something serious I want to tell you."

He looks at me solemnly. I'm confused by his serious tone and expression. When people get ready to say something they've been keeping to themselves, the mood is always like this. Suddenly, I feel as if the world had left me behind. Even so, I still have to ask him.

"What? What's wrong?"

He opens his mouth and closes it again. He pauses, like he's mustering the courage to say what he has to say.

"I found out my heart might not be very strong, and…"

I feel like the scene I've been looking out at is dimming before my eyes.

2

June 9 (Monday)

Morning at home: as usual.

Homeroom: Announcement about finals. Teacher jokes around (nothing worth noting).

First period break: Talked with Izumi about last Saturday. About the picnic at the park. She made our bento, so I said next time I'll try to cook something. She laughed and said she'd rather I didn't. How rude!

Second period break: Izumi went somewhere. Probably to the library. Suzuki asked what I was doing after school. I was vague, said I had to do something. She seemed a little annoyed. Had fun chatting about gaming livestreams, which she likes (make note in "People" section of binder). Saved the situation?

Third period break: Talked to Izumi about how I'm growing apart from Suzuki. She said I still have her, which made me feel better. I smiled and said, "Yes, that's true." She joked that it's not easy to catch a woman like her.

Fourth period break: Talked with Izumi. She said, "Wow, June sure crept up on me." I tried to joke about how everything creeps up on me. She said I'd made the same joke before, thought that was funny. Better make sure not to say it again (make note in "People" section of binder).

Lunch: Ate lunch with Izumi. She had a homemade BLT. Drool.

Fifth period break: Izumi is obsessed with black tea lately. Apparently, she likes Lady Grey, which Earl Grey created for his wife. I want some, too. Also, I never realized Earl Grey was the name of a real person.

After school: Izumi said she doesn't have to help her mom so much anymore, so she asked me what I wanted to do together. I suggested various things: riding a bike together, going to family restaurant, game center, karaoke, aquarium on our day off, amusement park. She said okay to everything other than riding on a bike together.

Then, even though she said she didn't want to earlier because it's illegal, she suggested we do it. As usual, she's up for anything.

We found an abandoned bike in the parking lot. Izumi said she'd fix the flat. Managed it with no problem.

We went to a country road far away from school where no teachers or police would see us and rode on the bike together. It was fun. The wind was really strong. I feel happy just remembering it. Ah, youth! It's like the hopelessness I felt this morning never even existed. I'm amazing. I'm impressive. I'm so glad I'm friends with her.

Even if I have memory loss, maybe I can enjoy each day like I did today. Riding together was a little scary, and this weird laugh came up from the pit of my stomach. She laughed, too. After we rode as much as we wanted, we walked the bike back to school.

She asked what I wanted to do tomorrow. She said we could ride the bike again if I wanted. She doesn't mind doing the same thing two days in a row.

The one good thing about the current me is that new stuff is always new.

No matter how many times I've done it, I enjoy it just like it's the first time.

I feel a little more optimistic than before. Izumi, thanks for today.

Before heading to prep school, I look through some of my high school journal entries on my laptop. I don't know how many times I've read the entry from that day. Sadly, I have no recollection of the things I wrote about, but it still makes me feel good to read them. There's no question that the living, breathing person in the journal is me.

I have a secret I haven't told my friends at prep school.

For about three years, starting at the end of April in my second year of high school, I had a problem with my memory. Every night when I went to sleep and my brain began processing my memories, it would erase them instead of storing them. There have been other cases like mine, but there's no cure. The only way to recover is to rely on the natural healing power of the human body. It seems that the younger you are, the stronger it is, and about three months ago, in April, I recovered from my amnesia.

In other words, I can remember what happened the day before.

Before that, when I woke up each morning, I couldn't recall what had happened the previous day. The fact that I still managed to graduate from high school surprised me and gave me hope for the future. Still, the anxiety was there.

Every morning, I would read the notes and journal I kept on my laptop and learn, for that day only, about my current situation and what had happened since my accident.

Through those entries, I understood that it was thanks to the devotion and self-sacrifice of my parents and Izumi that I was able to graduate from high school and attend art class a few times a week, which I'd given up before my accident.

When I had amnesia, I couldn't retain memories that consisted of information, but it seems I was able to store something called "procedural memories," which are rooted in physical sensations. I used my procedural memory to improve as an artist, and after graduating from high school, I spent the better part of each day drawing. Sometimes I hung out with Izumi, too.

According to my journal, the day before I recovered from my amnesia, I spent most of it drawing. I was able to draw the lines I wanted to and was able to instinctively capture the form of the people and objects I was drawing. That brought me a fresh kind of happiness, and it moved me.

Still, I feared going to sleep that night. Of course, if I didn't sleep, the next day's me would pay for it. I lay down, frightened, and slowly, I lost consciousness.

The next morning, when I woke up, I thought, *Oh, I fell asleep after all*. I had a slight feeling that something was off, but I ignored it, since that's a typical way you can feel when you wake up.

I got out of bed, feeling the sun on my face. Apparently, I used to get up really early in high school, but after I graduated, I started getting up with the sun.

With sleepy eyes, I looked at the notes taped to my wall.

I've suffered memory loss in an accident. Read the notes and journal on my laptop.

But I graduated from high school. I worked hard for that.

Put my heart and soul into each day.

Don't forget to be grateful for my family.

As I stared at the notes in a daze, I realized why I felt odd when I woke up. I should have forgotten everything—but I remembered what happened the day before. The fact that one day connected to the next, which, for most people, is completely normal, was unfathomable.

There was a knock on my door, just like there had been the previous morning. It was my mom. When I answered, she came into my room and gave me a strange look as I stared at the notes on my wall. I turned to her, unsure of what expression to make.

"Mom, with my amnesia, can I usually remember things for a little while when I wake up? Right now…I can remember yesterday really clearly."

Mom's eyes widened, and she didn't say anything. Apparently, this had never happened before. She ran out to get Dad. I felt confused, but I started going over the previous day's events in my mind one by one. When Dad arrived, the three of us talked about the day before. My memories were accurate.

They thought maybe it was because I hadn't slept well and told me to go back to sleep. It was hard enough for me to go back to sleep on a normal day, let alone when I felt so nervous and excited. I doubt even a sleeping pill could have put me to sleep.

Mom suggested we go to the hospital and started getting ready. Dad said he'd call the office and tell them he wasn't coming in until the afternoon and left my room. I told him he didn't have to do that, but he wouldn't listen. He said it was important, and he wouldn't take no for an answer. He must have been fairly flustered because he normally wouldn't say something like that.

In general, Mom and Dad are very level-headed, but they couldn't contain their excitement that day, because we ended up arriving at the hospital half an hour early. We waited in the car until it was time for my appointment. The doctor came in, and we explained to her the current development. She confirmed my memories of the day before with Mom and Dad. She did a complete exam, too, although she said it wouldn't tell us much. In the end, she told us to monitor the situation and come back the next day.

On the car ride home, Mom and Dad were both happy. They must have glimpsed a ray of hope. We still didn't know if I was recovering, but Dad said, "Everything will be fine" and smiled cheerfully. His words aside, now and then I saw him gripping the steering wheel and looking off into the distance like he was trying to endure something.

The next day, Mom and I returned to the hospital. I was able to remember the previous day and the day before that. It was the same the next day and the next and the day after.

"I can't make a definite judgment yet, but Maori seems to be recovering from her amnesia," the doctor said. Mom covered her mouth with her hands and turned away. She was crying silently. I'd never seen her cry before.

I called Dad and told him what the doctor had said. He laughed and said, "Didn't I tell you everything would be fine?" At the end of the call, though, I could hear him crying.

I told Izumi, too. She was in her second year at a national university in our prefecture by then. She came to my house right away.

"So it's like you said over the phone? Your amnesia is gone?"

"Yes! I did it! I did it, Izumi. It doesn't seem real at all. I feel like it's all some enormous practical joke. I mean, just a few days ago, I was in my second year of high school. But time has passed, that's for sure. Now they say I'm in recovery," I said excitedly.

For a second, Izumi looked regretful. Or maybe I imagined it, because the next moment, she was smiling.

Since then, I haven't lost a single day of memories. I got it into my head that I wanted to go to university, so I started going to prep school. You can say it was a gap year.

Aside from the weekends, I go to school every day. I'm working hard to catch up. Still, now and then I feel shaken by the vestiges of something, so I read the journal I kept on my laptop when I had amnesia. Just now, I was reading an entry from high school about when Izumi and I rode a bike together on a country road. Ah, youth…for two girls.

It was thanks to her that I was able to enjoy my daily life. I can't even describe what a good person she is. She spent her days catering to my wishes, or maybe I should say my selfish demands.

Apparently, the phone I had in high school broke, so I don't have any photos or videos from that time. Still, I have my journal.

I'm so grateful to Izumi. Without her, there's no way I could have graduated. She believed in my new life and pulled me along with her through the end of high school. I go about my present life full of unending gratitude.

When I wake up in the morning, I check to see if I can remember what happened the day before. I eat breakfast, get ready, and take the train to prep school. I've made some friends there. We complain and laugh together. I'm able to take those ordinary things for granted again. I've just gotten a little older. Sometimes at night, to give myself a break from studying, I draw.

I used to take drawing classes, but I wasn't good enough to apply to art school. Which is fine. I'm happy with drawing for my own enjoyment.

Time passed, and the leaves began to change color. One Sunday morning, I found a sketchbook in my room that I didn't recognize. It was behind my bookshelf, like it had been hidden there. I was tidying up during a study break, and that turned into a major cleaning spree of my room. Otherwise, I'd never have found it.

I took it out to the veranda and dusted it off. As I flipped through the pages, I came across drawings of a guy I didn't recognize. The moment I saw him, a stabbing pain shot through my chest and my heart pounded.

What was going on?

I closed the sketchbook. My heart was still beating fast. I could hear it thumping in my ears like it was desperately trying to tell me something. I thought about the sketches. They were drawn in my style. In other words, the past me had done them. The fact that I didn't remember them was proof that I'd done them when I had amnesia. Then why had I put them behind the bookshelf? I sensed something moving beneath the surface, but I couldn't bring up the memory. I must not have wanted anyone else to see the drawings.

What would I not want other people to see?

Maybe...drawings of a guy I liked or something.

I smiled at the ridiculousness of that idea. There was no way I could have fallen for someone when I had amnesia. Even now, for some reason, I had no interest in dating. There were all kinds of guys at prep school, some of them popular and good-looking. However, even when they talked to me, nothing inside of me shouted *Wow, nice, I like this guy*.

I opened the sketchbook again. The boy in the drawings looked a little weak, but very kind. Strangely enough, there were lots of pictures of him looking to the side and smiling vaguely or shyly but none of him facing forward.

As I gazed at them, my heart started to pound again.

Who was this person?

I'd read my journals many times, and I didn't think he was ever mentioned. Perhaps my mom would know, but I felt embarrassed about asking her. Maybe Izumi? I thought about snapping a picture on my phone and sending it to her, but I planned to see her in the afternoon anyway. Why not just show her then?

With that plan in mind, I returned to gazing at the boy in the sketchbook.

3

"I found out my heart might not be very strong, and…"

When Kamiya said those words, my mind went blank for a second. Then, when I realized he wasn't the type to joke about something like that, I was at a loss for words.

"I-is that so…? But it's not like anything bad will happen right away, will it?" I responded, trying and failing to brush away the seriousness of what he wanted to say. He smiled meekly.

"No. I'm just talking hypothetically. Actually, yesterday, I fainted. I must have been tired or something."

He said it happened with no warning. He had been with Maori at the library the day before, as usual. On the way home, he said he was on his bike and suddenly felt short of breath. He pulled over to the side of the road and was trying to calm himself down because he thought it was weird, when his legs suddenly became weak. He tried to prop himself up by holding on to the bike seat but ended up falling over with the bike.

When he woke up, he was in a hospital bed. It seems a passerby had seen him fall and called an ambulance. It sounds flippant to say, but the diagnosis was simply that he fainted. He regained consciousness quickly. There was a chance it had been caused by a heart condition, so he was supposed to go back later for tests. The sooner the better, and someone had to accompany him. Based on the hospital's schedule, he made an appointment for two days later. In other words, the day after he talked to me.

"Since my mom died suddenly from a heart condition, I had a lot of examinations done when I was younger. They didn't find any specific congenital disease. But my dad is still really worried, so they're going to run some tests tomorrow," he explained.

I remembered him mentioning that when he talked of his childhood before, but this was the first time I'd heard him talk about his mom. I tried to answer in a casual tone and finally managed to get the words out.

"Interesting. Um, if there's anything I can do, please don't hesitate to ask. Of course, I'll only do things I want to do," I joked.

He smiled faintly. Speaking of jokes, I once told him to be careful so that he didn't burn out and keel over one day. I don't think it's possible for words to create reality, but I was still shaken.

Kamiya was silent for a moment, like he was searching for the right words. Suddenly, his face grew very serious.

"In that case…and I'm only saying *if* something happens, and the chances of that are basically zero. I just want to ask you while it's on my mind. I'm not saying this is going to happen to me, but people do suddenly die sometimes."

"Um, wait a second, Kamiya. What are you saying?"

A cold, dry wind blew through, and I felt like it chilled me all the way to my heart.

"If I die, I want you to erase me from Hino's journal."

All thoughts vanished from my mind. I simply stared at the kind human standing in front of me.

If Kamiya died…

"But she keeps her journal in a notebook," he went on. "And I think she summarizes the important parts in a separate binder, too. So it's kind of going to be a hassle. You'll need to transfer the contents of the journal and binder to her laptop, only erasing the references to me."

A powerful emotion surged in me, words bubbling to the surface.

"Wh-what are you talking about? What is going on?"

I looked fearfully into his eyes. They were clear and calm, like they were detached from the rest of the world.

"This is important," he said.

"I don't want to do that. You should do it yourself."

"You're right. I should. I'm sorry to ask something like this from you. But I want you to listen."

"I don't want to," I said unreasonably. He smiled ruefully and continued.

"I hardly had any interactions with Hino before she lost her memory. So…if I die, as long as I'm not in her journal, we can make it like it never happened."

His words reminded me that something similar had happened before. It was when Maori had become emotionally unstable. We convinced her to erase those days from her journal.

"I think it might be possible. But are you okay with that?"

What person would want to vanish entirely from their partner's life? He looked at me with a sad smile.

"I think I'll be okay with it. We could say we broke up, but she might look for me. And I feel like if she discovered I'd died, it wouldn't be good for her mentally. That's why I think it's probably best to erase me altogether, even if it takes some work. Make it like we never even dated."

What he was saying was so sad, I couldn't help looking down.

"But you… I'm sure you won't die. You'll be fine."

"I know. But I think it's kind of a miracle that people exist at all. I mean, think about it. We're not like industrial machines. There's no outline or master craftsman to make us. We grow in our mothers' wombs, and from the time we are born, or sooner, actually, we're alive. I think it's miraculous. We're not robots built from a blueprint. If we have an abnormality, we might not realize right away, and if we stop working, it's not like we can just change out the broken part. The truth is, I don't fully understand what it means to be alive. It's strange and at the same time completely terrifying."

He looked down at the left side of his chest. In retrospect, I think I should have said something to him then. Like, "Do you really think doing that would make Maori happy?" Or something.

Yet I didn't because I felt there was some truth in what he said. Just a tiny bit, but it was there all the same. There was the possibility that Maori would fall into depression, and her parents were always worrying about…

"I'm sorry to bring this up," he said, smiling at my silence. He checked the time. "I'd better get going. See you later."

He walked off, leaving me with only a faint smile.

The following night, Tooru Kamiya died suddenly from heart failure.

I learned of his death that same night from his sister. I wanted to know how his tests at the hospital had gone, so I called his cell phone. I didn't get an answer, and since he'd told me once that he didn't check his phone very often (though I'm not sure if that was true), I gave up and hung up. About half an hour later, I got a call from his number. I picked up, relieved to hear from him.

"Hey, cell phones are for carrying around, so how about carrying yours? Anyway, how did your tests go?" I said.

"Oh…the tests didn't turn up any abnormalities," said a voice that wasn't Kamiya's. But I'd heard it somewhere before.

"Um, where is Kamiya?" I asked.

The clear voice answered sadly. "Kamiya…I mean, my brother passed away suddenly from complications with his heart."

It was just after nine at night. I felt like my room was expanding infinitely, and the ground swallowed up my feet. Kamiya's sister was saying something.

It seemed he had collapsed in his home roughly two hours earlier and died. As I listened to her talk, my mind plunged into profound confusion. How could someone die so suddenly? A person who, just the day before, had been standing close enough to touch?

His sister said she would tell me more the next day. We arranged to meet at three in the afternoon and hung up.

I listened to the waves of sorrow washing over my consciousness, and at some point, they became the sound of my own heart. In this world filled with loss, I was unprepared to face death. On the other hand, Kamiya, who had lost his mother unexpectedly, probably wasn't. I had been so surprised by his words the day before. And then…

Although it was pointless, I started looking up sudden heart failure on the internet. I was shaking. If I didn't do something, I felt like I would be consumed by frigid chills.

A number of conditions can cause sudden death in individuals who appear otherwise healthy. Sudden cardiac arrest is one of them. It can happen to anyone, anywhere, at any time. It kills far more people than car accidents, in Japan accounting for approximately sixty thousand deaths a year. This equates to one person dying every 7.5 minutes.

Although heart exams are widely carried out in elementary and junior high school, many cases nevertheless occur during class. Over the last ten years, over three hundred students have died suddenly in class, and the numbers are even higher for deaths out-side of school...

Recently, there has been wide recognition for the need of AEDs. Many have been installed at railway stations and public facilities, but they are not available at home. With each minute that elapses before treatment with an AED, the chance of a life being saved falls by 10 percent. If more than ten minutes pass before an ambulance arrives, chances of survival fall by over 80 percent.

I stared emptily at the lines of text. Suddenly, Kamiya's words came back to me.

I think it's miraculous. We're not robots built from a blueprint. If we have an abnormality, we might not realize right away, and if we stop working, it's not like we can just change out the broken part. The truth is, I don't fully understand being alive. It's strange and at the same time completely terrifying.

Like a miracle. Then had Kamiya's miracle come to an end? My eyes grew hot and filled with tears. I put my head down on my desk and wailed like a little girl.

The next afternoon, after some hesitation, I went to Maori's house. Ever since her accident and learning she had amnesia, she'd been avoiding hanging out with any friends besides me. She had various reasons for this. For one, it would be hard to answer texts from lots of people every day. On top of that, they were all steadily walking toward their future, and there was a chance each brand-new Maori would feel saddened from watching them get farther and farther away.

Our high school teacher knew about her amnesia, so it was unlikely she would hear about Kamiya's death. But he was in her journal. At some point, she would notice his absence. Especially since I had been friends with both of them, I felt I had to tell her what had happened.

"Kamiya…Tooru Kamiya is my boyfriend, right?" she asked when I did.

I looked down. She continued in a sad voice.

"I can't believe it. I-I've only read the summary in my journal so far, but I was so looking forward to seeing him today. He seems to be a very important person in my life…"

As I continued to stare at my feet, I heard her trying to hold back a sob. I looked up. She was crying. Her face was distorted with grief, and tears were falling from her big eyes.

"I don't know why I'm crying," she said. "It's strange, isn't it? I don't think I have any memories of him. It's so weird. I can't stop crying. Even though I've only seen his face in pictures. The only things I know about our relationship are from my journal. But here I am sobbing. It's so strange."

"Maori…"

I couldn't think of what to say, but I wanted to answer her.

"It's not strange, although I don't know how the two of you thought about your relationship," I said.

I took a deep breath to stop the pain in my chest. Kamiya would never feel this pain and suffering again. Why did it have to be him? Why? Why, when he was so kind? Why? Desperately, I kept talking.

"You two were made for each other. It had nothing to do with whether you could remember or with how many years you were together. Because the two of you truly loved each other."

I couldn't continue. I started to cry again. After that, Maori asked me about Kamiya, and I told her. I told her how much he cared about her and what they were like together and where they hung out. The more I talked about him, the harder it became to bear his absence. Still, time moved steadily forward. We decided to go see Kamiya's sister together.

With uncertain steps and thoughts, we took the train to his house. I rang the bell, and his sister answered. I had seen her picture in magazines and online, and we had talked the day before, but this was the first time I met Keiko Nishikawa in person.

She invited us to come in and sit down at the kitchen table, where we had often had tea with Kamiya. She said that his father, who I'd never met, was out taking care of some things. When I asked about Kamiya, she said his body was being kept at the hospital as they prepared for the wake and funeral. Then, slowly but in a very clear voice, she told us about the events leading up to his death.

She had gone with him to the hospital for his tests. In the year and a half since winning the Akutagawa Prize, she had appeared in the media many times. Her next novel was published in January of that year to positive reviews. The fact that she had made time to go with him to the hospital amid all this showed how worried she was. Early in the morning, the hospital staff had explained the type of tests he would be taking. The examinations lasted until the afternoon. Although the formal results wouldn't come back the same day, the staff told them they had found no obvious abnormalities in his heart.

After the tests, the two of them returned home. Their father came back from work earlier than usual, and Kamiya's sister told him they didn't find anything. He was relieved, and Kamiya relaxed in the bath, having skipped taking one the day before. When he got out and went into the living room, his father and sister were cooking dinner together. Kamiya watched, smiling. His sister asked why he was grinning.

"It's nothing, really. I just thought it was nice," she told us he said.

She told him to go rest and went back to cooking dinner. Suddenly, she heard something fall over behind her. She and her father turned around and saw Kamiya lying on the ground. She hurriedly called an ambulance and performed CPR, but he didn't respond. The ambulance arrived and tried to resuscitate him, but he never regained consciousness. Twenty or thirty minutes later, he was declared dead at the hospital.

The sound of the clock hovered among the three of us. None of us could move. I don't know how much time passed.

"Actually, I know a lot about the two of you," his sister finally said, looking first at me and then at Maori.

I dry swallowed and asked, "Did Kamiya…did Tooru talk about us?"

"Yes, he talked about you a lot, and he was always happy when he did. I met Maori once at the fireworks display in the neighboring district. Has your anterograde amnesia improved at all since then?" she asked Maori, who was looking down. We both widened our eyes in surprise.

"How do you know about my memory loss…?" Maori asked.

She looked confused. Kamiya had told his sister about Maori's condition. Maybe that was only natural within a family. However, Maori didn't know that Kamiya knew about her amnesia. I held my breath as his sister continued.

"I'm sorry. I don't know exactly why, but Tooru knew about it but pretended he didn't."

"I…I…kept it a secret from Tooru. So h-how did he…"

Maori went on to tell us about their relationship, including some things I didn't know. For instance, that Kamiya had confessed to Maori to protect a friend. That there were certain conditions to their relationship. The third of which…

"But Tooru truly fell in love with you. At least, as far as I could tell," his sister said. For a moment, Maori was speechless.

"I don't know. I don't remember. I really do forget everything. If I didn't have my journal, all the time I'd spent with him would be as if it had never happened."

She spoke haltingly and painfully, but she kept going.

"But he gave so much courage to the me of each day. He said, 'I'm going to show tomorrow's Hino a good time.' It saved me over and over again. The truth is, I was looking forward to seeing him today so much…but…"

She looked down again, and his sister let her words sink in.

"Thank you for telling me that. But it's no one's fault that you can't hold on to your memories. Tooru knew that when he dated you. I'm certain he enjoyed being with you. When I saw him with you at the fireworks, I was surprised. I never knew that he could fall for someone in that way. If he was able to think of you in his last moments, I think that would have made him happy. Thank you. Truly."

I waited for Maori to calm down, then asked Kamiya's sister the time and place of the wake that night. After that, we left.

My mind was still in the state of profound chaos it had been in since the night before. I was trying to decide if I should do what he had asked of me or not.

I was the only person in the world who could carry out his wish.

I went with Maori as far as her station but then said I had to talk to his sister about something and returned alone to Kamiya's house. I was worried about her emotional state, so before I left, I hailed a taxi to take her home. I told her I would meet her later and said goodbye. When I rang the doorbell at Kamiya's house for a second time, his sister answered with a startled look on her face.

"What's the matter? Did you forget something?" she asked.

"No, it's just, there's something Tooru asked me to do. And…I can't decide on my own. I wanted to ask for your advice."

She must have sensed my desperation, or perhaps the mention of her brother's request caught her attention, because after a short pause, she nodded and said, "All right."

I sat down at the kitchen table and told her about Maori's journal and binder and her risk of developing depression. I also told her that Kamiya had asked that I erase him from the journal and binder. When I was done, his sister sat there thinking for a while.

"If you bring me the binder and the journal, either the real things or copies, I'll type them into the computer. I should be able to patch up the spots where I remove him. I'm good at that sort of thing," she said.

I didn't know what to say.

"Do you think it's the right thing to do?" I asked.

I still didn't know how I felt about it. I probably would need to explain it to Maori's parents. But…if I did it, Kamiya would vanish entirely from Maori's life. If I didn't, she might suffer every day.

"I don't think it's up to me to decide if it's right or wrong," Kamiya's sister said. "The world is made of words. People cling to those words. Anything can be right if you think it is. And anything can be wrong if you think it is. That is the case here because the outcome is uncertain. Maori may suffer if you don't erase Tooru from the journal. You may suffer, too, if you see her and wish you had done as Tooru said. On the other hand, if you do erase Tooru from the journal, it may help Maori. Though, your conscience may be guilty. At this point in time, however, all of that is uncertain."

I listened silently as she went on.

"If living life as it's presented is the fundamental reality of human existence, then I believe it is right that either Maori suffers in her life or we suffer in ours from guilty consciences. But…Wataya, Tooru entrusted this to you. So you must decide. The only basis should be whether you want to do it or not. I will follow your decision. If you can't decide yourself, then you can use me as a reason. I want to fulfill Tooru's last wish. But…"

She looked down, her words trailing off. I felt as if I was on the verge of sinking into my own gutlessness once again.

In the end, I left without deciding and went to Maori's house. She was lying on her bed as if she was sick. I imagined what the next day would be like for her. In the morning, she would wake up and learn that she had amnesia. She would learn that she had a boyfriend who died and all that remained was her journal recalling happier days. Every morning, she would be confronted with those two absurdities: her own amnesia and her boyfriend's death.

There was the risk she would spiral into depression. If all she did was face each day with pessimism…

No, I had to stop. It wasn't right to use her condition to justify my own actions. Like Kamiya's sister had said, it came down to whether I wanted to do it or not. I'd always boasted about that, hadn't I? I'd always said I only did what I wanted to and didn't do what I didn't want to.

If I told Maori beforehand, I was sure she'd stop me. She wouldn't hesitate. For that reason, I decided to act on my own. If I was going to do it, I should do it as soon as possible.

I knew where she kept the binder and journal. She couldn't stay in bed forever. When she went to use the bathroom, I opened her drawer. Steeling myself, I stuffed the binder and journal into my bag. When she came back, I told her I was going to the convenience store and left.

I made copies of the journal, which took up several notebooks, and the binder and put the copies into envelopes. By the time I got back to her room, it was growing dark outside. If she had noticed the binder and diary were missing, I planned to make up an excuse. I was going to say I took them temporarily because I thought it wouldn't be good for her to read them in her state.

She said nothing. She was lying right where I'd left her and hadn't even turned on the light. It seemed unlikely that she'd tried to read the binder or journal. I'd taken a while making copies, but she didn't seem to think that was strange, either.

It was an odd time for it, but I'd bought some snacks, so I suggested we have tea. We still had the wake to get through. This was going to be a long day for both of us.

Maori stood up listlessly and left her room, saying she was going to the kitchen to prepare the tea. While she was gone, I returned the binder and diary to where I'd found them.

We left early for the wake to make it by the instructed time. When we arrived, I casually slipped Kamiya's sister the envelopes with the copies in them. I spoke to Kamiya's father for the first time and found him much more collected than I'd imagined from Kamiya's descriptions. He held back his own sorrow to fulfill his role as the resolute father. When he saw Maori, he bowed deeply, seeming to have realized something. I knew they'd met once at the fireworks show.

"Thank you for coming. I'm certain the deceased…I mean, Tooru is happy you are here."

I think I was probably the only one who noticed the drops falling to his feet.

When it was time to offer incense, Maori stood in front of the open casket, shaking as she stared at Kamiya's face.

The next day, I went to her house before noon because I was worried about her. She looked depressed. It seemed she had written about Kamiya's death in her binder and diary and had read the entries that morning. The day before, I had decided not to prevent her from writing about what had happened. I knew it was wrong, but I wanted to see what she was like without my interference. I wanted to know how she would react when she learned that her boyfriend was dead. She was haggard to the point of looking like a walking corpse.

In the afternoon, I went alone to see Kamiya's sister. Apparently, his father was busy with the funeral arrangements, having told his sister to leave everything to him. She had stayed up the whole night typing the contents of the binder and diary into her laptop. Rather than simply erasing references to Kamiya, she skillfully substituted me for him.

In reality, Maori and I were in different classes in our third year of high school. She changed that to say we were in the same class, like we had been the previous year, and smoothly adjusted the references to various people.

After she explained all of this to me, she asked me to review it to make sure nothing seemed unnatural. I said I would, and she went to Tooru's room to lie down for a while. I'd been surprised that I hadn't seen her cry and thought she must be emotionally strong, but now I could hear her muffled sobs through the walls. It made my own sorrow deeper. Tears spilled down my cheeks. This wasn't the time for me to cry. I remembered the work I had to do and wiped my tears.

I read through the new diary alongside Maori's original version. Every entry in the original held memories of Maori and Kamiya. I could practically see the two of them laughing happily in the pages. Kamiya—no, Tooru—had supported her so much. Thinking about it made me start crying again.

4

Within several days, Tooru's funeral was held, and I was done checking the diary. Without telling Maori, I talked with her parents and Kamiya's sister about what to do next. Maori's parents had known about Tooru since before his death and were deeply grateful for him and sad that he was gone.

Tooru's sister tried to buy Maori a new phone, saying it was Tooru's last wish, but Maori's parents insisted they wanted to buy it. In the end, they split the cost. After they bought it, I kept it with me.

In Maori's current phone, Tooru was there—in photos, videos, messages, and even in her text exchanges with me. We had to buy a new one to erase all those traces of his existence. We decided her parents should tell her they had to get it because her old one broke. We'd write the same thing in the new digital version of her journal and notes. As for the messaging app…we'd say we messed up the data transfer.

It was the morning of the third day after Tooru's funeral. I'd arranged with Maori's parents in advance to visit her room early in the morning. Since she was still weak, she was sleeping in her parents' room at her mother's suggestion.

I breathed in the quiet morning air and opened the desk drawer in Maori's room. I gathered the binder and numerous volumes of her journal and placed them carefully in my bag. I set her laptop on the desk, turned it on, and transferred the digital journal and notes Tooru's sister had given me to her computer. His sister had created entries for the days since his death as well. Using a certain program, she even falsified the time stamps on the folders and documents. Starting today, Maori would read the digital version of her notes and journal to learn about herself and her daily life and add her own new entries there as well.

Her old phone was plugged into a charger on another table. I took out the new one, intentionally messed up the data transfer, and registered her on a new messaging app. Now she wouldn't be able to see our past messages that referred to Tooru. She would no longer find any trace of her life with Tooru anywhere.

If that happens, I'll leave the rest in your hands.

I thought of that joking exchange with Tooru. Reflexively, I looked up. *Tooru, this is what you wanted, right? That reminds me, I never felt comfortable enough to call you by your first name when you were alive.*

I set the new phone on the desk and put her old one in my bag. I planned to keep it for her. She had lots of sketchbooks. I carefully tore out the pages with drawings of Tooru and tucked them into the large folder I'd brought with me. Then I went back and cut out the torn edges that remained in the sketchbooks.

I didn't think I'd forgotten anything, but just to be sure, I looked over the checklist I'd written. I *had* forgotten something important. I had to change the notes taped to the wall. I looked them over.

I've suffered memory loss in an accident. Read the notes and journal on my desk.

But I graduated from high school. I worked hard for that.

Put my heart and soul into each day.

Don't forget to be grateful for my family.

They were mere sheets of white paper, not the kind of things that have souls, but they had watched over her day after day. I couldn't bear to look at them for long. I felt as if I was violating them.

I've suffered memory loss in an accident. Read the notes and journal on my laptop.

I was only changing one, but since she might become suspicious if one looked different from the others, I switched them all for sheets I'd typed and printed from my computer. I knew every word by heart.

As I worked, I discovered there was a sticky note on the back of one of her notes. When I read it, I froze.

Even if I recover, always remember Tooru Kamiya. The impor-tant things will always be in an important place.

Why was it on the back of the paper? I couldn't help wondering. My best guess was that she had put it there so she would see the words when she took them down…in other words, when she recovered from her amnesia.

I didn't think she had noticed what Kamiya's sister and I were doing, but she must have sensed something was going on. Or was it simply an expression of her strong feelings for Tooru?

I felt like I was going to cry. Regardless, I had to keep this for her, too. If I stuck the sticky note onto the back of the new sheet, she would probably discover it eventually.

I put the paper in my bag with the sticky note still attached. Then I taped the printed sheets up on the wall. I turned off the lights, but before I closed the door, I looked back one more time. The new, lifeless slips of paper stared back at me.

From that day on, Maori's daily routine took place on her laptop. She read her digitized notes and journal there and typed in new entries. Her mother told her she'd always done it like that.

I went to see her the day after the switch. Although she didn't know Tooru had died, she nevertheless seemed to be suffering. She didn't know why she felt so off.

"I guess the data transfer for my messaging app failed," she said glumly. "It sucks. They reminded me of how much fun you and I had. Now I can't look at them."

I wrapped my arms around her in a hug.

"It'll be okay. We'll do even more fun stuff starting now. Not just in texts; in real life. I...I'll make sure your tomorrows are fun, okay?"

She seemed confused by my uncharacteristic response, but eventually she said, "Okay" and rested her face on my shoulder.

"Thanks, Izumi," she said.

Over the next two or three days, she gradually recovered. The human ability for self-healing made me happy and sad at the same time.

April arrived, and Maori settled into her new routines. Soon enough, the old Maori was back. Although I was a university student now, I tried to see her on the weekends. On weekdays, she took drawing classes in town and went for walks in the park. Sometimes I would see her walking near the station alone. In the past, she had always been with Tooru. Something crucial was missing, but she didn't realize it. Seeing her like that broke my heart.

On a warm day at the end of April, she and I went for a walk in the park. It was the place where she and Tooru had gone on their first date, and where the three of us had picnicked under the cherry blossoms the spring break before our third year of high school. Maori had asked that we go there. As we walked among trees that had already shed their last blossoms, she spoke haltingly.

"It's hard to explain...but I feel like I've forgotten something very important. I just can't remember. I guess that's only natural, considering my memories disappear every night."

A little less than a year later, Maori recovered from her amnesia. She enrolled in prep school, and the months passed until it was fall. Now she was sitting across from me at a café with a sketchbook filled with pictures of Tooru and a question for me.

"Do you know who this is?"

Several thoughts swirled in my mind. Why was she holding a drawing of Tooru? I thought I'd collected them all, but I must have missed this sketchbook.

I took a sip of my water.

There was no need to hide the truth about Tooru anymore. Maori no longer had amnesia, and the risk of depression associated with it was gone as well. If I told her about Tooru, she would get past it in time. She would feel some pain, but I was sure it would heal.

"Oh, him? He's just a guy you saw a couple of times at the library during summer break in high school."

All the same, that was how I answered her question. I didn't know what was best for her. She had completely forgotten Tooru. Even if one day she looked through the sketches again and sensed something odd, maybe she would have a boyfriend or a husband by then and forget all about it...

Maybe there was happiness in that, too, and there would be no need to unearth the sorrows of the past.

She wasn't satisfied with my answer, though, and began searching within herself for a better one.

"But why are there so many drawings of him?"

"You were just getting into drawing portraits. You wanted to have a guy to draw instead of just me all the time, and he offered to help."

"I never saw anything about that in my diary. And why did I hide the drawings? I found them behind my bookcase. Now that I think about it, I used to hide important things there when I was younger."

A place where she hid important things? I remembered the message on the sticky note.

Even if I recover, always remember Tooru Kamiya. The important things will always be in an important place.

I finally understood what it meant. It wasn't metaphorical. The important things really were in an important place. In other words, she meant to tell herself never to forget Tooru.

"You know how overprotective my dad is," she said. "In elementary school, he used to sneak into my room and read the group journal I kept with my friends. I hated that, so I started hiding things behind my bookcase. He finally stopped in junior high, and I forgot all about the hiding place. I found this sketchbook back there. I don't think it's a coincidence."

She pouted, like her curiosity was mixed with dissatisfaction.

"Izumi, are you hiding something from me?"

It's not that I'd never predicted this day would come. I could brush it off with a laugh. If necessary, I could make up a story to explain it. There were all sorts of options at this stage. Having said that, I wasn't so sure what to do.

Before I realized it, my vision was blurred with tears. I could see how unsettled Maori was. I told myself not to cry. Why was I crying? Why would an eccentric person like me be crying? A person whose thoughts didn't even make sense? A cold person like me? Just smile and make up a story. Then this would all be over.

"Maori, that guy…"

But there was no way I could lie to her.

"He was your boyfriend."

The two of them loved each other too much for me to lie about this.

Maori made a bewildered sound. I desperately tried to keep talking. I could see Tooru's face in my mind. Smiling vaguely, troubled, that serious face of his from the last time I saw him, when he entrusted his request to me.

"But, Maori…" I choked, unable to even wipe my tears away.

"He's…no longer in this world. He died."

An Unknown Girl
and Her Unknown Boy

1

When Izumi told me about the boy in the sketchbook, confusion overwhelmed me. Meanwhile, she was talking about my relationship with him. She told me that our first odd encounter, which you might call a coincidence, turned us into a fake couple. That we saw each other every day. That each day's me gained strength and became more optimistic because of him. That I had him to thank for picking up drawing again.

And that suddenly, one day, he died due to a heart complication.

She also told me that his last request was to erase all trace of him from my journal.

I was in shock.

I wasn't angry at Izumi or Kamiya's sister. I was in a vulnerable place, and they did what they thought was best for me. Also, it was his last request. If I was in their position, I'd probably do the same thing.

But I was appalled that I forgot all of it. I was speechless at the realization that I'd so easily forgotten a person I cared so much about.

Izumi apologized over and over, and I kept telling her she shouldn't worry about it. Even so, my mind went blank, and I couldn't wrap my head around it. Izumi seemed worried about me and said she was going to get something. I nodded. My eyes fell on the sketchbook. I'd had no idea the guy in the sketches was my boyfriend. Even when I saw the drawings, the memory didn't come back to me. But…maybe my body and heart remembered him. Maybe my heartbeat was desperately trying to tell me something.

I picked up the sketchbook and flipped through the pages. The pictures showed him with different expressions. I still couldn't remember him. Even though he meant so much to me, and I never should have forgotten. My eyes grew hot, though from sadness or regret, I wasn't sure. There were many versions of him before me. Yet I couldn't remember.

I sat there in a daze for some time. After a while, Izumi came back. I forced myself to smile. She nodded and, with a sorrowful expression, held out a stack of notebooks, binders, and a big folder filled with drawings.

"These are the real journal and notes you wrote and more pictures of Kamiya. The diary will tell you everything about your time with him. I'm sorry. I should have told you right away after you recovered. I'm so sorry for keeping it from you these past months and for depriving you of your most important memories."

I told her she didn't need to apologize and took the stack from her. I considered reading it then and there but realized I might start crying and decided not to. She was looking down guiltily.

"Izumi, at least eat something. Eat something sweet."

Finally, she looked up.

"What?"

"You have absolutely nothing to apologize for or feel guilty about. Words can't express how grateful I am to you. Thank you. I mean it," I said.

Partly to cheer her up and partly to mollify the waiter as we sat in that café for so long, I ordered a ton of desserts. I ordered a smoothie made with seasonal fruit, the usual shortcake, chestnut chiffon cake with whipped cream, and Izumi's favorite, chocolate cake. Sweets always cheer us up. Izumi's tense expression began to soften as we ate and bantered. I made a lot of jokes to lighten her mood.

"I guess when I had amnesia, the new items on the menu were always new to me," I said, grinning. Izumi was kind enough to do the same, even if it was a little forced.

"You used to make that joke all the time," she said.

"I know," I answered. We smiled at each other like we always did.

Back home, I gathered my courage and opened my diary. The whole story, from the day we met until his death, was there in my own handwriting. I could tell as I read it—this person named Kamiya was always by my side, always treating me with care, always trying to fill my days with joy. I had described his subtle habits, his interests, and his attention to "being sanitary." I had written about how he smiled faintly when something troubled him. I couldn't read everything in one sitting, but through my writing, I sensed his living, breathing being.

The binder had a special page labeled "Tooru Kamiya" that was also full of information about him. As I sat there engrossed in the notebooks and binder spread before me, twilight fell, and my room grew dim. My mom came up the stairs to tell me dinner was ready. I said I wasn't feeling well and would eat later. She hesitated, then said, "I heard you learned about him—about Tooru Kamiya."

I was surprised she knew, but she said that Izumi had called to tell her. Through the door, she told me not to blame Izumi. She said that Izumi and Kamiya and his sister had all struggled, but they had done what they thought was best for me.

I opened the door and looked at her.

"Mom…did you know him?" I asked.

She cast her eyes down and shook her head.

"I wish we'd met. We never got that far. But…your father and I are still deeply grateful to him. On the anniversary of his death, we always visit his grave, although we kept it secret from you, of course. There's no question in our minds. He is the person who believed most in your future and protected your heart."

Mom was crying. Crying like she did the day my amnesia went away.

Then she pulled herself together, wiped her tears, and smiled. "Let me know if you get hungry," she said kindly and went back downstairs.

After I shut the door, I sat on my bed and hugged a pillow. The darkness outside was deepening. I tried to concentrate, but my thoughts were too scattered. The minutes ticked past.

Moonlight shone into my darkened room. I wanted to remember something in that stillness. I prayed that I would.

A little after eight, my phone lit up. It was a message from Izumi saying she had my old phone and that she'd charged it and could give it to me whenever I wanted. I wondered if seeing photos and videos of him would help me remember a little. I almost accepted her offer, but in the end, I didn't.

Thank you, I texted back. *Maybe if I saw the photos and videos, I'd be able to remember him. But I feel like it would be a bad idea. If I looked at them, the image of him that I already have might be blotted out by the image in the pictures...and that scares me. I might only be able to remember the version of him in those photos and videos. Maybe I'm being silly. Sorry.*

She texted back: *No, I'm sorry. I think I understand what you're saying. How about just listening to his voice?*

I hesitated but ultimately agreed to her suggestion. A few minutes later, she sent me an audio file she'd extracted from a video. I clicked play and heard something rattling and then my own happy squeals. There was the sound of the wind. Gradually, I remembered when this was recorded.

It was the day I'd insisted we ride a bike together.

I heard myself again. Could I really have laughed so innocently and joyfully? And could I really have forgotten it?

"Hino, you shouldn't lean forward like that. You'll fall off."

There was another voice. Kamiya's. Tooru Kamiya. The guy who was my boyfriend. His voice sounded oddly calm for a high school student. I answered happily.

"I'm fine! You're just a worrywart."

"You're just a daredevil."

"What? I can't hear you over the wind!"

"Nothing."

"Tooru, thanks for another good day."

"What? Did you say something?"

"Nope, I didn't say anything."

The recording ended. My whole body was shaking like it was reso-
nating with the past.

In the stillness of the night, I listened to the recording over and over.

2

Starting the next day, whenever I didn't have prep school, I visited
various people to ask them about my relationship with Tooru Kamiya.
I contacted my classmates from the past and told them about my
amnesia and recovery. All of them were shocked. And they all said the
same thing about me and Kamiya.

"The two of you always seemed to be having so much fun together.
At first, I was surprised to hear you were dating, but when I got used to
it, I started to think you just might be perfect for each other. It was cute
the way you always called him 'my boyfriend' or 'Tooru,' but he always
called you by your last name."

Maybe word spread that I was asking around, because one of Kamiya's
classmates from second year got in touch, and we ended up meeting.

"I was actually the reason the two of you started dating," he said.
"Or my bullying, I should say."

He was a serious kind of person whose white button-down shirt
seemed to suit him. He didn't seem like the type who would have bullied other kids, but then again, that might be true for every former
bully. He explained what had happened, not glossing over the truth,
but while recalling it all, he sounded pained. He told me how Kamiya

had spoken up for another kid in their class and how he came up with a dare on the spot.

Apparently, the guy had excelled at sports and academics in junior high and been quite confident. Once he got to high school, though, his grades started falling, and he became depressed. He turned into a bit of a bad boy. Then, partly because he became isolated after the incident with Tooru, he started rethinking his life and studying harder. He even moved up to Izumi's advanced class in his third year.

"I… The name of the guy I bullied was Shimokawa. He transferred to a school overseas, and he's still over there. He actually launched his own start-up even though he's still in university. When I heard Kamiya had died, I knew I had to contact him. He rushed back from China for the funeral and cried louder than anyone else there. I'm pretty sure he knew about you."

He told me Shimokawa's full name, and I was able to find his information online right away. He came across as an intelligent, well-educated man with a handsome, toned face.

Izumi introduced me to one last person who had known us. Tooru Kamiya's sister.

Meeting someone I'd only read about in the journal made me nervous. She would remember me, but I'd forgotten her. I was able to get a sense of her personality through the entries. I made my way to the café in a hotel attached to the terminal station downtown where we'd arranged to meet. I told the waiter the name the reservation was under. He led me to a seat in the back. Kamiya's sister was already there. When she saw me, she stood up.

"Hello," she said before I could greet her. Embarrassed, I hurriedly bowed.

"H-hello. Thank you for making time to meet me today. And thank you for coming here when I really should have gone to you."

"It's all right. I had an errand nearby, so it really was no trouble," she answered, sounding like the novelist she was.

She gazed at me. She was a beautiful woman. I sensed a refined gentleness and a quiet intimacy in her. Suddenly, her expression softened.

"You've recovered from your amnesia?"

"Yes. Thankfully. And I…," I said, looking down.

She gestured for me to sit. We both sat at the table, opened our menus, and ordered drinks. When that was done, she resumed gazing at me like she was thinking about something.

"Actually, I've said this before, but thanks to you, I know that Tooru was happy."

I forgot to blink as I thought about the meaning of her words. He was happy. Could that really be true? He had stayed by my side until the day before his death. Yet I had lost all my memories of him. I had lost them, every single day. Our past together wasn't really mine. All that remained was the journal and binder.

"I don't remember Tooru," I said.

"I know. But that doesn't change the fact that Tooru was happy," she answered.

Our eyes met. I thought I glimpsed something like sadness in her eyes.

"I think his time with you gave color to his life. He's gone now. But the person he loved was you. You were the one he cared about and the person he wanted to make sure was always happy," she said.

My chest tightened. I pressed my lips together. From the corner of my eye, I saw Kamiya's sister looking down.

"I'm sorry…I know that was sudden. But I don't intend to tell you I wish you could remember Tooru. On the contrary, I want you to forget Tooru and start a new life. That was the future he was trying to protect. Possibilities. I want you to put him in the past, to be your own kind self, and to make another person happy. You have the ability to do that. You can reach out and claim happiness for yourself. I want you to live like that. And I'm certain Tooru wanted that, too."

She was talking about my future. I couldn't help thinking about the people who had believed in my future even when I had amnesia. Izumi, my mom, my dad. She herself, I'm sure. And…

"Is that really all right? To forget him?" I spat out, thinking of the face in the sketchbook. His sister looked at me with clear eyes. She smiled, maybe to reassure me.

"Yes, it is. People live by forgetting."

"What about you?" I asked.

She looked into the distance. Just then, our drinks arrived. She gazed into the amber liquid in her teacup and took a stip. I did the same of my coffee.

"One day, I think Tooru will slip into the past for me as well. If I'm still writing novels then, maybe during interviews I'll mention him by accident. He'll become a person from my past. No wound vanishes completely, because wounds are also memories. But the pain won't last forever. I think that's how life works. Although, I'm sure I'll still remember him when a nostalgic wind blows or I happen to type the character for his name in a manuscript."

Wounds remain, but the pain doesn't. I suppose that's the way people survive their sorrow. Do they grow less sad with time? Maybe. You can't walk forward if you're forever a prisoner of the past. Yet it made me sad to think that one day I wouldn't be anymore.

"Memories are important, aren't they?" I said. His sister looked at me questioningly. "I've lost that. If everyone else is gradually forgetting him, then I want to gradually remember. I want to try to get back what's important to me. That's how I feel."

His sister knitted her eyebrows in consternation.

"It might be painful," she said.

"I want to remember for myself. Everything important ought to still be here inside me."

"Can you promise me you won't become a captive of the past and that you won't neglect your own life?"

"Yes."

"Someday, someone…," she said, then paused. "It's a bit bold of me to say this, but one day, when a person who loves you comes into your life, love them with all your heart. Put Tooru behind you."

I still didn't understand love. At the same time, I couldn't help remembering the descriptions in my journal of my time with him. What should I call that? Youth? Love? He didn't want any reward. He simply gave and gave. Every day, asking nothing in return…

"I promise I will. Of course, that all depends on a person like that showing up," I said, smiling sheepishly. She smiled back gingerly.

It was the first time we had smiled at each other. After that, I asked her a lot of questions about Tooru. What kind of child was he? How was he raised? She answered slowly, searching for the words.

"I'm finally able to read your book and remember what I read from day to day," I told her as we talked. She smiled, looking very beautiful. When I asked what she was writing now, she hesitated before answering.

"It's a serious story but not without redemption. A story about a boy and a girl. Perhaps if they hadn't met, they would have lived out their individual lives happily enough. However, through meeting, they found greater happiness and meaning. That's what it's about."

Starting the next day, I made sure to prioritize my current life, just as I'd promised Tooru's sister. I kept up with my studies, but at the same time, I began trying to remember him. My present was the future he had created.

Fall ended, and winter came. I studied furiously and managed to pass the university entrance exams. Although it was my second choice, I got into a university in the prefecture. I would start that spring, two years later than my classmates. I wonder how Tooru would have reacted if I told him. Would he have been happy for me?

On a sunny spring afternoon, to celebrate my acceptance, Izumi and I had a picnic beneath the cherry blossoms at a park that was famous for them. We'd been there a few times before. The early-blooming trees rustled in the breeze. It was still a little cold when the wind blew. We ate Izumi's homemade bento and walked around the park. She poured a black tea from her thermos into a paper cup and handed it to me. The aroma was fruity and refined.

"I feel like I remember this smell," I said casually, looking at the blossoms. Izumi stopped walking.

"Maori...you said that once before."

"Did I? When?"

I could tell from the way she hesitated that it was when I had amnesia. She told me the story. It was in our second year of high school, when we went to the aquarium.

"Kamiya ended up running into his sister, so the two of us went to the aquarium alone. We took the bento he had packed in a rattan basket with us. He'd made this beautiful *chirashizushi* with lots of toppings, and he included this tea because he thought it would go well with the rice. When we drank it, you said it seemed familiar. Actually, he'd made it for us once before at his house."

She went on to explain that the sense of smell is connected to the hippocampus, which processes memories and emotions. For that reason, smells sometimes evoke memories. After she finished talking, I looked down at the amber liquid. A petal fell toward it but drifted to the side instead. I wondered if I would always be like that petal, so close to remembering him but ultimately unable to. It had happened before, where I felt like I almost remembered something only to have it slip away.

"Is that so?" I answered absently and took a sip of tea.

I'm going to show tomorrow's Hino a good time.

Without any reasoning or knowledge, someone's voice rose from my pool of memories. It caught me off guard. The voice was so clear. Was my mind reading out lines from my journal in the voice I'd heard on the audio file Izumi had sent me?

I don't expect happiness. And that's fine with me.

No, that wasn't it. Those words weren't in my journal. I saw a faint smile. It was blurred so I couldn't see it well. But still…

Until I met you, I thought that's all my life would be.

I recognized the face. It belonged to a pale, thin, kind person.

Every time I say your name, I get a thrill.

The person who mattered so much to me. The person who always made me smile.

Is it okay if I fall in love with you?

The voice stopped. I was in a daze, and for some reason my eyes felt hot, and my vision blurred. A soft wind blew, tearing the freshly opened blossoms from the trees.

"Can I say something?"

I turned around at the sound of Izumi's voice. She was looking worriedly at me. I bit my lip to keep myself from crying.

"Yes. Thank you. Just now…I started to remember something."

"You did?"

"I heard a voice. He was laughing. He said he would show tomorrow's me a good time. At least, I think so."

She seemed to know right away who the voice belonged to. She looked down sadly, but I smiled. Still, my voice was shaking.

"I don't remember anything. But I'm alive. And one day, I'll remember it all. Just watch."

"Okay."

"Everything important is here inside me. I'll remember all of it, every last thing. I know I will. I…I…"

I covered my face with my hands. No matter how deep our sorrows, humans eventually forget. Wounds don't hurt forever. I remembered what Kamiya's sister had said, but as long as my wounds did hurt, I would keep crying. That was fine by me. Who cared if I was a crybaby?

It was all mine. The sorrow, the pain, the joy, the memories, all of it. When I thought about that, I started crying again.

My Heart Will Draw
Your Portrait

1

Cherry trees are blooming here and there on the road from the station to the park. The sun was shining strongly this morning, but after noon, it weakened. The mild rays cast a pale light on the people and plants in the park. Cherry blossom season is here once again. For the first time in ages, I'm strolling along with nowhere to go in a hurry, gazing at the city scenery around me.

Not long ago, I was in high school. Hounded by university entrance exams, I thought my third year flew by faster than any other year in my life. But my first year as a working woman went even quicker. Amid these hectic days, high school feels like the distant past. Sometimes, I wonder if it was all a dream. Maybe none of it ever happened. Maybe I'm still in high school, passed out from exhaustion after studying. When I open my eyes, I'll see Maori or Tooru smiling and be reassured by the sight of them being happy together, giving me a peace of mind. Unfortunately, that's not reality. I'm twenty-four already.

I don't remember anything. But I'm alive. And one day, I'll remember it all. Just watch.

Three years have passed since Maori said those words to me with such determination. She's in her fourth year of university now, and she's still trying to remember Tooru. Using her journal and my stories as a guide, she's gone to the places they visited, done the same things, and desperately tried to remember.

It didn't work like the Lady Grey tea. Things didn't go so easily or simply. Nevertheless, she kept looking inside herself, never giving up. Even in university, she kept searching for her own forgotten past. Little by little, she remembered Tooru.

Now that I'm working, I can't see her very often, but we still try to see each other at least once every three months. This sunny Sunday is one of those times. We've arranged to meet at the park famous for its cherry blossoms, where we've been a few times before. It's already crowded. She and I came here when she got into university, and during spring break before our third year of high school, we came here with Tooru.

"Izumi! Over here!"

As I walk through the park searching for her, I hear her bright voice calling me. There she is, sitting on a big picnic blanket in a spot with a great view of the flowers. She said she wanted to try choosing the spot herself at least once and didn't mind holding down the fort as time would fly by if she was sketching the trees. Even as she tries to remember Tooru, she's living her own life to the fullest. There are a few people sitting with her, probably friends from university.

"You look cheerful as always, Maori," I say.

"I'm a little creepy when I'm not cheerful," she jokes.

I think of the day I told her Tooru had died. That, too, is far in the past.

She introduces me to her friends, and we all help ourselves to the picnic dishes spread on the blanket. Everyone brought something, and

Maori brought homemade *chirashizushi*. She used to be an awful cook, but she's improved since then. It's different from when she and I made it before, when she was trying to recall memories of Tooru. This time it's piled with tasty toppings and looks beautiful.

At first, her university friends are reserved around me because I'm slightly older and already a working adult, but when I smile and talk to them, they warm up to me.

Little by little, I'm changing, too. All sorts of things are happening every day out of view. I think that's what it means to live.

I glance over at Maori. She's chatting happily with a friend. I wonder if her current life is what Tooru wanted for her. To take ordinary things for granted, have good times and bad times, a peaceful life. To fall asleep at night and wake up in the morning. Is her life now what he always believed it would be? A constantly evolving life, where in a few decades she'll be able to look back on the sad events of the past as one part of her story.

Wanting to talk to her alone, I suggest we take a walk along a path lined with cherry blossoms. She brings her sketchbook, saying she wants to draw the flowers. We banter for a while as usual, and then I ask, because I've been wondering about it, "So what happened after that?"

Maori stops walking. She doesn't ask what "after that" means. After a minute, she says "Well…" and holds out her sketchpad. I wonder what she's up to, but I take it. We go stand under a tree so we're not in everyone's way. I open the book. There are all sorts of drawings— landscapes, portraits, animals. Probably her daily sketches.

"Very nice, as always. But what's the point?" I ask.

"Well, I'm a little embarrassed to show you, but keep going," she answers.

What could she be embarrassed about after everything we've gone through? I smile and look up. Petals dance silently downward.

"The cherry blossoms are beautiful, aren't they?" I remark.

She glances up, too.

"They really do look like snow. Snow that never knew the sky, was it? I read that in my journal. We came here together, didn't we? And he told us about the poet who called them that."

I look at her.

A poet once called cherry blossoms snow that never knew the sky.

Maybe to the sky, the scattering petals do look like snow that materialized from nowhere. Tooru had an oddly refined side to him, probably due to his sister's influence.

Maori must have read that journal a thousand times. I didn't remember the line until she mentioned it. Sadly, the passage of time has stolen my memories of Tooru. I close my eyes and pull up an image of him. He appears from the darkness, but his face is slightly blurred. It's sad how much he's faded in just six years.

"My journal also said something about how he taught us another meaning for May sickness, although there weren't many details. I wrote down that it was funny," she says, then falls silent.

I open my eyes and glance toward her. She still stubbornly refuses to look at the photos and videos of Tooru from her phone. She says that everything important is within her and keeps trying to remember. Sometimes, whenever I think of her struggles, I become sad. Even if she does remember him, he won't come back. Not ever. I press my lips together and start turning the sketchbook pages. She remains deep in thought.

"Oh, I remember," she finally says. "It was about how everyone is busy when the cherry blossoms are falling, but in May, things calm down, and…"

I come to a drawing, and my hand stops flipping through the pages.

The wind blows, sending up a storm of petals around us. I feel like I'm watching an emotionally moving film for the first time or stopping in front of a striking painting; a fresh feeling courses through me, moving relentlessly forward.

Tooru is there in her sketchbook.

Drawings of Tooru I've never seen before. In all the sketches of him in her old sketchbooks, he's looking to the side, frowning shyly or smiling faintly. But not the Tooru in these drawings.

These are pictures of Tooru as Maori remembers him.

I calm myself down and turn the page. There he is again, with the same expression. I lose myself among the drawings. There are many versions of him. They are exquisitely drawn, as if to proclaim that this human really did exist. I can almost hear his familiar voice.

I look up at Maori. She's staring at something. A row of cherry trees. I almost say something to her but then stop. I've seen her with this look before, when she was trying to recall something.

"Izumi, I'm sorry, but could I see the sketchbook for a minute?"

"Hmm? Oh, of course."

I hand it to her. She takes out a pencil and starts drawing beneath the flowers in full bloom. She draws quickly. I realize it's the first time I've watched her draw. I'm surprised by how fast the forms take shape.

Of course, it makes sense. She does it every day. She did it when Tooru was alive, and afterward, too. In minutes, she's completed her rough sketch.

Someone is sitting under a cherry tree. She fills in the outlines, and the figure comes to life. It's a drawing of Tooru on the day the three of us picnicked under the cherry blossoms. He's gazing at me with tenderness glowing in his eyes, with the exact kind look he had that day. No video or photo retains a trace of that look. Only someone who was there with him could draw it.

My vision slowly blurs. *Damn it*, I think, pulling out a handkerchief and dabbing my eyes.

Sanitation. You can't fake it.

You know something, Tooru? After I met you, I started ironing my handkerchiefs.

Suddenly, the time I spent with him replays in my mind like a fast-forwarded movie. All of it will be lost eventually. It will deteriorate and disappear. But…even if everything is constantly shifting, even if the process of continuing to live dims the souls of the beautiful ones, some things remain unchanged.

The world that our hearts draw never fades.

"I remembered something else about Tooru. But I'm sure I haven't remembered it all yet," Maori says, still sketching. She lets out a long breath. "I loved him…and he's gone. But the memories are here inside me. Sleeping here in my body and my heart. By remembering him, we can continue to live together. I can't explain it very well, but it's similar to hope. The world is gradually forgetting him. But…"

A tear falls from her eye. She wipes it away and begins to draw again.

"I don't know why I'm crying. Maybe I'm still hurting. Except I feel warmth, too. I think I still love him. But it's all right. I'll fall in love again one day. I'll reach out for happiness. Until then, just a little longer…"

I want to say something, but maybe words aren't needed right now.

Tooru is here in this world of constant loss. He lives on inside of Maori, and in her memory, that's the expression he's making.

In all her drawings of him, he's smiling.

He's still there, smiling like he did that day, watching over her with those kind eyes of his.

Afterword

Just as death is a part of life, we lose all kinds of things even as we gain others. Only when we lose them do we understand their true value.

Health is one example. When we get a cold and feel unwell, we realize how important our health is. Relationships are another. When we lose them, we learn how precious they were.

Some things can be recovered, but some can't. Although we only have one chance at life, by the time we notice our losses, it's too late.

At a certain point in my life, I realized that the things I take for granted today will one day be gone. That doesn't mean I'm a pessimist. Imagining future losses makes me value things in the present even more.

One day, I may lose all contact with the people I work with today. The thought makes me want to value our time together and our relationships more deeply and to be kind. One day, I may grow apart from the friends I spend time with now. So I want to appreciate them and enjoy our time together with all my heart. Not even our dearest family and friends are here forever. It changes how I think of them.

The main characters in this book lose important things they once took for granted. It's a sad story but not a tragedy.

Many people helped this book reach publication. For all the support I received, I am beyond grateful. In particular, I learned much from my editor. I look forward to continuing our relationship in the future.

I would also like to express my sincere gratitude to all my readers. I can't thank each one of you individually, so allow me to bow my head in appreciation for all of you here. Thank you for reading this book. I hope our paths cross again somewhere in the future.

MISAKI ICHIJO